Octave Thanet, E. V. Wilson

Tales from McClure

The West

Octave Thanet, E. V. Wilson

Tales from McClure
The West

ISBN/EAN: 9783744661010

Printed in Europe, USA, Canada, Australia, Japan

Cover: Foto ©Andreas Hilbeck / pixelio.de

More available books at **www.hansebooks.com**

Tales from McClure's

"IT WAS PROVOKING TO HAVE LIZZIE LOOK SO SERIOUS."

Tales from McClure's

THE WEST

TOWN LOT No. 1303
By Octave Thanet

BARB'RY
By E. V. Wilson

THE HOME-COMING OF COLONEL HUCKS
By William Allen White

A POINT OF KNUCKLIN' DOWN
By Ella Higginson

THE SURGEON'S MIRACLE
By Joseph Kirkland

DIKKON'S DOG
By Dorothy Lundt

THE DIVIDED HOUSE
By Julia D. Whiting

NEW YORK

DOUBLEDAY & McCLURE CO.

1897

CONTENTS

TOWN LOT No. 1303

BY

OCTAVE THANET

TOWN LOT No. 1303

.↙.

EVERY breeze that blew waved and in-
flated and tossed the white flag with
the red map of Arcadia addition to the town
of Bloward, which hung over the center of
the main street; nor did it any the less flutter
and interlace the red ribbons decking four
white horses and eight brown, bay, or sorrel

horses. The white four drew a band-wagon, wherein sat the band, glorious in red cloth and gold braid; the two darker fours drew similar wagons, filled with those who figure in the rear of processions as "citizens and others." Possibly the "others" are women; at any rate, they seemed to be of that sex here. It was a crowd more than good-natured —hilarious. Jokes having the peculiar twang of Western humor were bandied .about, so that a constant din of laughter

blended with the ring of trowels from either side of the street. Turn how one would, he could see brick walls rising.

"The boom's struck Bloward, an' don't you forgit it!" said the president of the Arcadia street-railway, proudly waving his umbrella at arches, gables, Renaissance turrets, Early English buttresses, and a motley company of terra-cotta bedizenments, friezes, parapets, and finials on the new façades, which looked, amid the cheap wooden shops and dry-goods-box architecture of a former day, as if they had strayed into the town and did not know the way out. "How's that for building?" he cried, lunging his umbrella enthusiastically into the eye of a passer-by. "Beg pardon, ma'am. Oh, Mrs. Crowe! Going out? Oh, plenty of time. Now, there's a woman's made most fifteen thousand dollars in real estate this last year—jest a woman! Old Rolfe's made thirty, an' Curwin an' Bragg as much again; an' T. J. Wheelan—why, there's no counting *his* profits. Great Scott! you cayn't stake out the lots fast enough. Children cry for 'em. Why, look at the situation—six railroads, and strong indications of natural gas. There ain't a question 'bout it; we're

bound to double up here inside five years.
Going out?"

The man to whom he spoke hesitated.   He

was a slight, modest-looking man, the youth-
fulness of whose fresh skin and confiding

smile were rather belied by a high brow from which his hat had worn the hair too soon, and a few wrinkles above the bridge of his nose. His neat coat had been deftly rebound with new braid, but a suspicious gloss shone on the sides, and his boots were patched.

"I—I was n't thinking of it," said he; "my wife is rather expecting me—"

"Supprise with a town lot— Ah, there, you!" The busy man was away amid the crowd, waving his umbrella.

Now Augustus Plaintiff knew perfectly well that a clerk in a hardware store, with a salary of fifteen hundred a year and a wife and two children, has no business speculating in town lots. But there was a hundred dollars in the savings-bank, and somehow— it seemed to Gus without conscious volition of his own—the crowd pressed him forward, and the next that he knew he was in the wagon, jammed between Mrs. Crowe and Mr. T. J. Wheelan, whose profits there was no counting. Gus glanced sidewise at him; this man during a few months had made more money than he had made in his whole life.

7

Yet he had been saving, hard-working, honest, faithful. He thought of the lean acres in the Vermont farm where he was born, of the unending drudgery in heat or cold. Then he thought of his wife and the two boys— Gus, nine, and Sammy, three (there was a little grave out in Vermont: she came between Gus and Sammy); and he thought of the hundred dollars in the savings-bank. To think how hard it came! how Lizzie had scrimped and pared the household expenses —no meat to-day, no milk yesterday, a dyed gown, darnings innumerable, hours filched from sleep to iron and clean and mend for Mrs. Crowe, "the second-hand woman" (so the boys called her), who had rooms next to theirs—good heavens! how did the woman manage, anyhow ? He thought what a sweet, rosy face Lizzie had when they went to school together. He remembered that he used to picture how, after they were married, he would buy her a black silk gown and a gold watch. She should have a lace collar and a coral pin. Those days her lips were red as coral, and her brown hair had a glint of gold

8

in the curve of its waves, and her violet eyes
sparkled so bright—so bright in the twilight.
Well, now she was his wife. Her best gown
was the dyed black woolen, five years old that
spring, and the only watch in the family was
the silver Waterbury which, somehow, Lizzie
had earned enough to buy for him. He
thought (with a lump in his throat) how
cheerful and loving and patient she had been.
This hundred dollars in the bank had an object.

The Plaintiffs lived above Mrs. Crowe's
"Blue Front Renovating Emporium." ("For,"
said Mrs. Crowe, "I ain't goin' to spend my
time cleanin' up clothes an' things, an' then
fault 'em as second-hand.") They had a room
for a parlor, but they had no furniture.
There had been a fire and sickness and doc-
tors' bills East, and railway tickets and furniture bills West, until the Plaintiffs' purse
was far too lank for parlor furniture. But
now the money was saved, and this dearest
delight of Lizzie's heart could be gratified.
Time and again the two had planned the furnishing: only two new chairs, for the red

wicker rocker was good still, and a cheap
table adorned with the scarf Lizzie had em-
broidered, and the black horsehair sofa which
had been mother Plaintiff's, and an ingrain
rug (Gus, after hours, could paint a border
on the floor), and perhaps curtains—curtains
on a gold rod. This afternoon being a half-
holiday, Gus was actually to have gone with
Lizzie to buy the articles which they had
"looked at" half a dozen times. Instead,
here sat Gus, greedily listening to tales of
fairy gold. Every sale made somebody rich.
There was to be a canning factory on Arcadia
addition; a Chicago firm was to build a vast
pork-packing house on the east half; an Eastern syndicate wanted to buy the land; natural gas had been discovered in the southeast
corner. Money seemed to float in the air,
for any one's clutching. The jovial buyers
told stories of recent investments. A sharp
fellow had made twenty thousand on a single
deal. A timid fellow had edged away with
hundreds, which his successor, of harder
metal, had turned into thousands. "What
you need is to keep your grip," said the street-

car magnate. Over Gus's head dangled a placard. Lots would be sold at prices ranging from five hundred dollars upward. "One fifth cash; remainder in two years, six per cent. interest." Why, he could buy a lot himself.

He glanced from Wheelan, who had apparently gone to sleep, to Mrs. Crowe, a wooden sort of a woman, whose nose was too long for her face, as her body was for her legs. Sitting she looked like a tall woman, but when she rose she became absurdly short. Her figure she herself was wont to describe as "all of a bigness"; literally, it was all of a thinness, and its straight lines were not disguised by any vain curves of drapery. "Got too many knobs and corners to ketch on fur furbelows," said Martha Crowe. Her black skirt hung in plain folds; there were no ornaments on her black coat; her black straw hat had a band of crape upon it like a man's. She wore her iron-gray hair short, saying, "Ain't never had 'nuff to waste hairpins on."

She rarely smiled, even behind a bargain;

but a kind of sardonic irony gave her talk an edge. She had not a visible creature in the world belonging to her, except an apoplectic old dog. Rumor explained her black garb as mourning for the departed Crowe; but as it was known that he beat her until she pitted the red-hot poker against his fist and drove him out of the house, this explanation was not accepted generally. Furthermore, Mrs. Crowe had an open grudge against the sex, which she gratified not only in words, but by lending money at an unconscionable rate of interest. Yet Lizzie Plaintiff always maintained to Gus, who had a great dislike for the woman, that Mrs. Crowe had her good points. "She always pays promptly, and she pays fair wages; and I don't believe a cleaner woman ever lived; the house is kept in repair better than any place I know." All the more Lizzie wondered over Mrs. Crowe's business. "How can you stand all these dreadful old duds?" she said to her once. And Mrs. Crowe had answered in her grim way: "You kin stan' dirt on dollar bills. It *pays*. But— well, 't is bad," she owned. "'T ain't so

12

much the clothes; the furnichure is what beats me." She gave Mrs. Plaintiff a glance of awful significance. "I dream of 'em nights," said she.

"For the land's sake!" gasped poor Mrs. Plaintiff, "you don't think they can walk upstairs?"

"Bless you, no. You ain't no call to fret. I got a solution that 'ud kill the wanderin' Jew. You kin buy every blessed thing I 've got safely, an' that 's more 'n you kin say of some of these big furnichure stores, too. I could just make your hair raise your bunnit, Mrs. Plaintiff; mother's, too. Some folks say they cayn't be killed. *I* kin kill 'em. They 's secrets in all trades, as a fool man I knowed used to say—but the only thing he ever did say war n't a lie. Guess *your* husband 's middling clever to ye?"

"Indeed he is," cried Lizzie; "he is the best husband in the world!"

"I came from your town," Mrs. Crowe went on calmly; "his father kinder kept comp'ny with me onct. Guess neither him nor his son would set the river afire. But he

looks clever. I would n't go without my
meat for dinner to save it up for his supper,
though, if I was you. You kin cut off your
right hand fur a man, an' then, like 's not,
he 'll grumble 'cause you 're left-handed.
Oh, I know 'em! I 've summered 'em an'
wintered 'em. You eat your meat."

Unfortunately, Gus, having come home
half an hour earlier than common, heard
every word of this speech, because he was in
the hall outside. Sitting by Mrs. Crowe's
side now, he wriggled in his seat under the
prick of those remembered sentences. Mrs.
Crowe turned her pale-green eyes on him.
"Thinkin' of buying?" said she.

"I 've not decided," replied Gus, coldly.

"Well, I would n't, then," Mrs. Crowe said,
without expression either in face or manner.
"Better go home."

"I guess if you 'd followed your own advice you 'd have been a good deal poorer,"
said Gus; and when a man opposite laughed
he felt a glow of satisfaction. His wits were
equal to this old harpy's.

"Well," said Mrs. Crowe, deliberately,

"that's different. I've got some money to fool away if I wanter, an' you ain't. I'm plenty smart enough and plenty mean enough to be a match for the real-estate booms goin' on forever an' ever, amen. It ain't—"

"Oh, I'll risk it," Gus laughed.

Mrs. Crowe, after looking at him a second, said, "Well, 't ain't none of my business."

Gus was tempted to reply that he agreed with her there; but on consideration that she was a woman, he forbore, though he chafed almost as much over her grim silence as over her words. To divert his thoughts he screwed his head round until he could look out on the landscape. Soon the scattering houses were passed. The muddy road cut a straight black line through a green sea of prairie. The talk and the jokes went on; the brass band played in front; the horses were of good mettle and trotted swiftly. Still Gus wondered if the addition was not rather distant from the town. At last they reached the stand for the sale, and the beer pavilion, and the flock of little flags standing sentries over the lots. There were no trees and no grass;

15

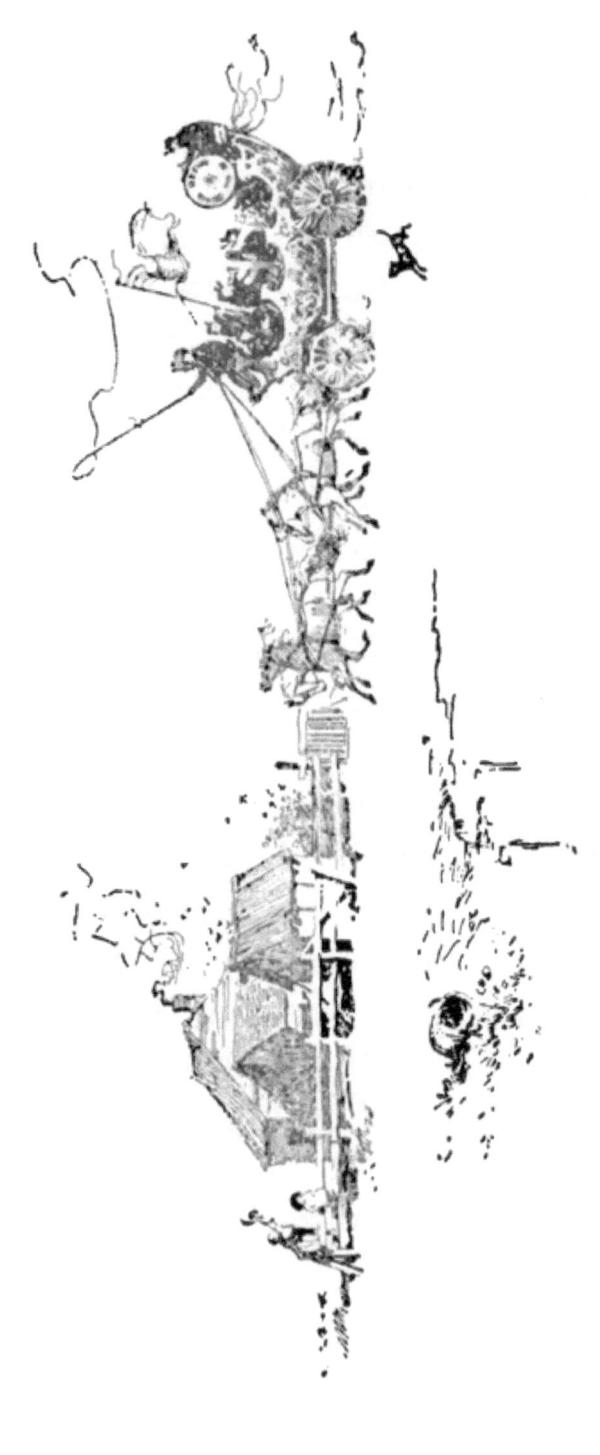

but pools of water glimmered under the huge dock-leaves, and there was a rank growth of plantain and jimson and smartweed, making the ground quite as green, from a distance, as grass would. Mr. Wheelan plodded through the mud, and Gus splashed after. The lucky speculator halted before a flag bearing the number 1303. Gus also halted.

"I suppose they will build up rapidly," said Gus. Wheelan made a motion with his shoulders between a shrug and a shiver. "You thinking of investing, young man?"

"Well, yes. Ain't it a good investment?"

"If you can afford to lose the money, young man, then you can afford to speculate in land; and you *may* make something if you buy right. But if you can't afford to lose, you better not touch it. You heard Mrs. Crowe. She's apt to be sound." So saying, Wheelan walked away.

"I'll bet he's just trying to scare me off 'cause he wants that lot himself," was Gus's instant thought. So readily do we impute deep-laid craft to other people's motives, and

17

GUSS AND SAMMY WERE TAKEN OUT TO VIEW THE
FAMILY ESTATE.

so seldom do we allow them to be swayed by
random impulses like our own! Ten minutes
later Gus was the owner of lot 1303, and he
returned home with the deed in his pocket.
He found Lizzie distracted with anxiety over
his long absence. Matters were not greatly
helped by the explanation. Lizzie grew quite
pale. "Gus—then—the parlor—" she stam-
mered, making a pathetic effort at conceal-
ing her disappointment; "but of course we
can wait awhile." If she had reproached
him it would have been easier, Gus thought.
He kissed her, and called her his precious,
brave little wife; and Lizzie, poor soul, for a
minute believed that such words were better
than chairs or curtains. He broke into a
fervid eulogy of the lots: "Directly on the
street-car line—"

"Oh, did you go out in the cars, Gus ?"

"Of course not—the track ain't laid; but
it 's right on the line. And there 's an Eastern syndicate, and parties from Chicago—"
The magnificent gossip of the wagon was repeated, until Lizzie's imagination caught fire,
and she reproached herself for her wicked

19

disappointment. Before they went to bed they had made no less than six hundred dollars. In view of such opulence, Lizzie herself did not consider a beefsteak for supper extravagant; she even allowed herself to be helped twice.

From thenceforth lot 1303 may be said to have become one of the family. They talked of it constantly. Gus and Sammy were taken out to view the family estate; in consequence, Mrs. Plaintiff spent the most of the night removing cockle-burs and mud from their garments. Sammy explained that, in their glee, they had "wrastled" and slipped. "Say, ain't papa real kinder happy all the time now?" said Gus. "He gives me a nickel 'most every Sunday."

"Yes, deary, but I 'd save 'em if I was you," said his mother; and for some reason she sighed.

She asked Mrs. Crowe to give her more work, saying she could find more time. She found it by rising earlier. "An' how 's 1303?" said Mrs. Crowe. "Sold it yet?"

"No; but Gus is offered seven hundred

dollars; but there is strong talk of the canning factory wanting it."

"Tell him to sell it if it's cash or a good man."

Gus nodded his head wisely over this message. "I guess I understand the old Crowe's little game by this time," he told Lizzie.

No. 1303 was bought in May. By June house lots in Bloward were quoted at double their May prices. "Only, I wish, Gus, they would pay the money down," said Lizzie; "they want to pay so little down, and give notes or swap property."

"You don't understand business, Lizzie. If we all paid down there would n't be money enough to go round."

In July 1303 was held at fifteen hundred dollars. Two lots adjoining it were actually sold to Eastern men for that price, cash. They belonged to Mr. Wheelan. "Crowe has sold five lots to the canning factory for a thousand apiece," Gus reported. "I had an offer of twelve hundred—two hundred down, and the rest in two years; but I told him it was fifteen hundred or nothing.

They 've found indications of natural gas."
However, Lizzie's pleadings were so strong
that he sought the buyer, no less a personage
than the president of the Arcadia railway,
and offered to sell.

" Humph," said Mr. Gault,—Gault was the
great man's name,—" I 've bought elsewhere.
You 're the day after the fair, my Christian
friend. But maybe we can fix a trade. Tell
you what: I 'll give you a thousand in Arcadia,—selling for one twenty-five on the
street now, but I call it par—and my note
for four hundred dollars for six months.
How 's that ?"

Thus it happened that Gus went home
with an announcement of the sale of 1303
for sixteen hundred and fifty dollars. He
was buoyantly delighted, talking of the new
parlor furniture and even a watch for Lizzie.
It was provoking to have Lizzie look so serious when he explained that there was n't
any ready money, exactly; she couldn't seem
to understand that the stock was just as
good. He really had a mind to sell a little
to give her a lesson in finance.

Chuckling over the vision of Lizzie when he should bring, say, six hundred or so dollars and fling the notes in her work-basket, Gus tried to sell his stock. But somehow he found no buyers. And somehow, though outwardly the boom was booming as uproariously as ever, though the real-estate bulletins bristled grandly with figures, and prices were stiff, and brass bands played in front of the real-estate offices, and the daily journals waxed eloquent over the town's prospects, underneath all this clamor was a sinister timidity. Nobody was buying. Within a month there was a general cautious retreat of the speculators. The retreat became a rout. At last Gus came home one evening, long, long after supper, and flung his head upon the table and groaned. He believed that Lizzie was in her chamber; but she was there in the shadow, waiting, and she came forward and lifted his head from the table to hold it against her heart.

"Let us bear it together, dear," said Gus's wife.

Then the man tried to straighten his

shoulders and hold up his head with a miserable assumption of jauntiness. "Oh, it's nothing. Just yawning. I'm dead beat, chasing round town after the scoundrel. Lizzie, Gault's gone—sloped."

"Run away?"

"Exactly. Canada, I guess, leaving a pretty mess behind him. The Arcadia's busted. Stock is n't worth a cent—no more than his swindling note. He has n't paid a dollar for 1303; all I could do was to get it back. He would have nailed me to make the payments, and sold it; but I was in time —though Lord knows how I'll raise money for the next payment, next month."

A little pause, during which Lizzie only stroked his hair, before she said timidly: "Dear, they say the boom is burst. Don't you think we better—we better let 1303 go, and not try—it will be so hard to raise that money, and more in another six months, and it takes so long for a boom to come back, and there are the taxes and the interest—"

A savage laugh stopped her, and Gus leaped up and began pacing the room. "I

tell you I cayn't do it, Lizzie. I cayn't bear
it. Maybe I'm jist flinging good money after
bad; but after the way I've worked and
hoped and planned, I cayn't *stand* it to see
that lot slip out of my fingers. The property's bound to come up, you know."

But it was one thing to resolve to make
the payments, quite another to raise the
money. How bitterly did Gus revile his
extravagance during the season of 1303's
fictitious prosperity! His smart new clothes,
his new hat, his cravat, were odious to him.
"You brute!" he accused himself, "while
your poor wife did not spend a useless
penny." He worked over hours to get
money. He stinted himself every possible
way. The peaceful evening pipe was sacri-
ficed; he ate a dry roll for his luncheon.
One morning he brought a bundle to the
emporium. Not only his new clothes and
hat, but his watch and Lizzie's cherished
table-cover, were spread on the counter for
Mrs. Crowe's lack-luster eyes. "Can you
give me fifty dollars for the lot?" Gus asked,
trying to keep the tremble out of his voice.

" Your wife know 'bout that there kiver?"

Gus was too wretched for retort; he nodded. The "second-hand woman" eyed him, not keenly, but in her usual expressionless fashion.

"She knows," said Gus, clearing his dry throat; "she—she gave me ten dollars; it's our second payment on the lot 1303."

"Guess you wish you 'd a-follered my advice."

Gus, mopping his brow, and his eyes glittering with anxiety, forced a sickly kind of smile. "Guess you 'bout hit it that time," said he.

"Well, why don't you foller it now? Let them sharks take their darned old weed-patch back."

A quiver ran over the young man's pale face, while he began to gather up the loose articles.

"Quit that. I s'pose you 'd go somewhere else if you cayn't git what you want. Well." She opened the till and took out five ten-dollar bills, saying, "There; I 'm a fool too, and that 's a pair of us."

Gus thanked her warmly; but she gave him no answer beyond staring at him through his faltering speech.

"Well, ain't I a fool!" he heard her remark to herself, as he hurried away.

Though he had the money, he was a wretched man. It humiliated him to take Lizzie's hard earnings. Worse than all, there was the insurance money. For years Gus had kept his life insured. The thought that if anything happened to him Lizzie would have a little sum to help her face the wolf had comforted him in many a hard experience. Now it would be impossible for him to raise enough by to-morrow to make the payment. "Oh, well, nothing is going to happen to me," said Gus, "and I'm bound to stick to 1303!"

He was impressed by the different appearance of the office when he went to pay his note. Dismally quiet were the rooms which had been so thronged. The few men lounging about read the bulletin boards and talked in an undertone, with frowns and significant nods and liftings of the eyebrows. While

Gus stood waiting for his receipt, and absently gazing out of the window, the number of signs "To Let" and "For Sale" which met his eye made his heart shrink. At that moment, if he could have got one hundred and twelve dollars (principal and interest) out of the hands of the affable young man with the diamond pin, he would have abandoned 1303 and fled. But the day of grace was past.

He went down the marble steps into the street. The first object to greet him was a notice of sheriff's sale tacked on to an unfinished building. Yes, the bomb had burst. Like an echo of his thought a tumult of noises rose behind him. Yells of "Take care!" "Look out!" pierced the clatter of wheels and the mad gallop of hoofs. But he never saw the peril—the heavy wagon, the frenzied horses, and pallid driver; they were on him before he could turn his head. The horrified people closed, in the wake of the runaway, over a trampled heap of clothes pulled from under the wreck of a wagon. Something like a dripping red blotch, with a black circle jammed over it, meant a man's head under his hat. The driver limped up presently. His first inquiry after his horses having been gratified by the sight of them with heads hanging, knees trembling, and standing in a cowed fashion at a little distance, he bethought him of the heap. Was he hurt much?

"Neck broke, that's all," came the answer.

Gus, feebly creeping out of a roaring blackness into the light and the sense of real sounds, heard every word. They were like hammer blows. Life is sweet even to the wretched; but it was not of life Gus thought: it was of Lizzie and the children, and the insurance policy which would lapse to-morrow. They heard him try to whisper; it was a name: "Mrs. Crowe, second-hand woman." That was the reason for Mrs. Crowe's presence at the hospital half an hour later. Wooden as ever, she stalked up to the cot and seated herself. The doctor and nurse were too much startled by her inexplicable height when she sat down to notice any change in her face. The patient was unconscious; he had not spoken since he pronounced her name. Mrs. Crowe, in her emotionless voice, told them to send for his wife and children—"In a carriage; I'll pay," said she. She indicated Gus with her thumb, looking the doctor in the eye: "Goin' to die?"

A voice from the bed answered her: "Yes, Mrs. Crowe."

"I did n't ask *you*," said Mrs. Crowe; "you don't know nothing about it."

"But I am. I 've been mistaken both times I contradicted you before,"—he tried to smile with his bruised, stiff lips,—"but I ain't now. Mrs. Crowe--Lizzie—the best wife—"

"Give him some brandy," said Mrs. Crowe.

He gulped the brandy eagerly. His eyes implored her before he had strength enough to say: "They won't have nothing. Will you—give me—enough money to pay the life insurance? It's due to-morrow. I'll give you 1303."

Mrs. Crowe was sitting bolt upright, as one would expect of Mrs. Crowe, a hand spread on either knee. She lifted these hands to pull her hat down over her eyes, and she frowned. Then she pushed back her hat, revealing a face like a blank wall. "'Gustus Plaintiff," said she, "I kep' company with your father 'fore I married Crowe. He was a fool jes' like you; but he was clever. I liked him better 'n he liked me. I 'll give you two hundred dollars for 1303; so you kin set your mind to rest 'bout the insurance. What ye goin' to die fur?"

"My neck 's broke. God bless you!" murmured Gus, somewhat irrelevantly, but with deep feelings.

"No 't ain't. Could n't swallow so slick 's you did if your neck was broke. You ain't going to die. That 's another mistake of yours. Young woman, lend me your handkerchief; my old dog died this mornin', an' I feel sorter upset."

With the most entire deliberation Mrs. Crowe wiped two tears away, and returned the handkerchief; nor did the doctor and nurse ever witness any other token of emotion, though she attended Gus with great devotion during his illness. It was tedious and for a while critical, but he recovered eventually. He grew to feel a queer kind of attachment for Mrs. Crowe. Lizzie made a clean breast of secret help received from the woman of wood. "And she grew kinder and kinder, Gus. She brought every one of those things you sold back, saying she only bought them because she knew you 'd sell them to somebody else. And I think, Gus, I do think the poor soul was fond of your father, and he did n't treat her just right, and it soured her. Money and smartness won't make up for some things to a woman."

"No," said Gus, musingly; "and we owe a great deal to her."

They have owed much more since—among other things, the furnishing of the parlor. It is even whispered that Mrs. Crowe intends leaving her savings to the Plaintiff boys. One thing she certainly will not leave them —town lot 1303. They too are aware of this, because on a certain evening when, as happens often now, they were all together, Gus took his courage in both hands and asked, "Mother Crowe, what have you done with 1303 ?"

The family interest had for so long clustered tenderly about that garden of plaintain and cockle-burs that they all felt a kind of a shock when she replied: "Oh, I bundled the deed right back to them agents! 'T wa' n't wuth the taxes."

BARB'RY

BY

MRS. E. V. WILSON

BARB'RY

Y ES, I was at his first wife's funeral; an'
if anybody had told me 'at in a little
more 'n a year I 'd 'a' ben his second I 'd
said they was crazy. You see, my third
cousin, Marthy Jane Holly, she thet was
Marthy Jane Spaldin', lived in his neighborhood, an' I was visitin' o' her when his first
died, an' Marthy Jane tuk me along to the
funeral. It was a dreadful dull day in Feb-
ruary, an' that muddy the team could hardly
pull us; an' when we druv up to the house I
thought it was jist about the lonesomest
place I had ever seen. The house was a
great big two-story frame, with nine winders
an' a big front door; an' the yard had n't a

tree or bush in it. "Law sakes, Marthy Jane!" says I, "what a barn of a house!"

"Well," says she, "it 's bran' new; they jist moved in it this fall."

There was a sight o' folks in the house, an' I got in somehow 'mong the women, an' tried to look 'round some, but I got sort o' interested in the talk. One o' the women said, "What a pity 't was Mis' Hillyer had to die jist as she got settled in the new house." An' another one said she 'd noticed many a time, when folks built fine houses, one or t' other of 'em died. Then a right old woman spoke up, an' says she, "That 's nonsense. Matildy Hillyer killed herself, so she did. Her an' them two slips of girls done all the work fer the men 'at built this yer house, an' for the hands 'at worked the farm; an' the las' time I see her she tole me she made a hundred yards o' rag carpet, wove it an' all."

"What made her?" interrupted another woman.

"Nobody made her," said the old woman. "She 's that bigoted. I tole her 't would n't pay; but she said squire was sot on hevin' the biggest house on the prairie, an' they got the work done cheaper by boardin' o' the men, an' she 's boun' to hev carpets—"

"I don't care," broke in my third cousin, Marthy Jane Holly; "it 's her own fault. Ef she 'd managed the squire right he 'd never built sich a house. She tole me she wanted a littler one, handy an' full o' closets, but the squire wanted the big one. Now I say ef she 'd managed—"

"Oh, pshaw!" said the old woman. "Mis' Holly, you dunno what you 's talkin' 'bout. The woman that 'll manage Sam Hillyer ain't born."

At this minit a man came to the door of the kitchen where we was sittin', an' said, "All as want to look at the corpse, please walk in." I went in with the rest, an' tuk a look at the pore critter, an' went on through the room where she lay, across a great hall, into another big room, an' I thought a hundred yards o' carpet would n't begin to cover all them floors. My! but they looked cold an' dreary; an' I said to Marthy Jane Holly,

when we got back to their cozy little house,
that it 'peared to me I 'd freeze to death
there.

Well, when my visit was out I went home,
an' I declare I never thought once of him;
but along about Christmas, what does Marthy Jane Holly's man do but come down to
our house with him in a sleigh! You might
'a' upsot me with a feather when they walked
in.

You see, I was nigh on to thirty-five, an'
not bein' extra good-lookin', I 'd 'bout concluded nobody 'd ever want me fer a wife.
But the long and short of it was, he had
heard about me, an' he said he was lonesome,
an' his children needed lookin' after—an' I
tell you he 's a good talker! An' Marthy
Jane Holly came to see me, an' said all he
needed was the right kind of a woman to
manage him; that he was a good pervider,
an' had about as good a farm as there was
in the county. An' my brother Jim, as I was
livin' with, an' Cynthy, his wife,—she was
Cynthy Smith, ole Tom Smith's daughter, you
know,—they said it was a splendid chance

fer me; they knowed I could get along with
him. An' so I give in; but I sort o' mis-
trusted that air sot mouth o' his all the
time. But, as I said, I 'greed to hev him at
last, an' we was married at brother Jim's
early in March; an' Jim an' Cynthy give me
a right nice weddin' dinner—I will say that
fer 'em; an', what 's more, I always will believe they thought it was a good thing fer a'
ole maid like me to git to be Mrs. Squire
Hillyer.

I felt a little jubious about his children
wantin' a stepmother. You see, the oldest
girl, Em'ly, was about eighteen, an' I thought
maybe she liked bein' boss. But laws! she
'peared glad when I come, an' had a real nice
supper ready; an' Barb'ry, the next girl, was
a-smilin' too; an' I heerd her tell the boys—
there was three of 'em, from fourteen down
to ten years old—that she liked my looks.

Well, I kin tell you, it was n't long afore
I found out that managin' him was no easy
matter; an' Em'ly was his picter. When he
wanted a thing done, it had to be done his
way; an' she was like him, an' so they did n't

agree very well; an' he hevin' the power, she hed to give up, an' so she was 'most always in a bad humor. The boys, too, especially Steve, the oldest o' the three, was everlastin' quarrelin'. So I begun to think, afore many weeks, that I 'd better stayed single, even ef it was n't pleasant livin' with sister-in-laws; an' ef it had n't ben for Barb'ry I dun know what I 'd 'a' dun. But Barb'ry—dear, dear! I choke up yet when I think o' her. She was so pretty, with her big blue eyes an' white skin an' red mouth.

I can't somehow help likin' good-lookin' folks, an' I do think it 's a real misfortune fer a girl to be ugly. Mebbe I 'm wrong, but I know I allays felt it was to me. An' the minit I see Barb'ry I liked her, an' the more I see her the more I liked her. She was that sweet in her ways, allays givin' up to Em'ly, an' a-callin' of me "ma" from the start, which is more than Em'ly ever has to this day. An' I soon see she was his fav'rite; not as he said so, but I could see his eyes follerin' her as she went singin' round the house; an' then, she never said nothin' back

44

to him, no odds what he said, an' Em'ly, pore
thing, never could hold that sharp tongue o'
hern. Not that she was n't right, often, an'
him wrong; but what 's the use o' bangin'
your head ag'in' a stone wall? I say.

I could n't help laughin' to myself a little,
fer all it hurt mighty bad, when I thought
o' Marthy Jane Holly and Cynthy talkin' o'
managin' him. I did try to better things at
first. There was so much hard work. You
see, there was nine in the family, countin'
the two hands, an' allays eight or nine cows
to milk, an' the chickens, an' the garden;
an' we women hed all them to 'tend ter; an'
I says one day, "Ef you 'd let the girls hev
part o' the butter money for theirselves,
don't you think they 'd like it ? Girls wants
a little money sometimes." He jist gimme
one look out o' them steely eyes o' his, an'
says he: "The butter an' eggs hes allays
bought the groceries. You better not be
puttin' fool notions in them children's
heads;" an' his mouth shet down like a rat-
trap, an' you better know I hushed up. But
I kept a-thinkin',—wimmen will, you know,

—an' I thought, "He calls 'em children. Well, I ken tell him they 're past that; an' ef I ain't fooled, Em'ly 'll show him pretty soon "—fer I 'd see her an' one o' the hands together a good deal. He was a nice enough young man, so I did n't meddle; what 'd ben the use? Well, after a while I found out 'at Barb'ry wanted a' organ awful bad, an' the school-miss 'at taught the deestric' school where the three boys went to school all winter hed got the spring term, an' wanted to board at our house, an' said ef Barb'ry hed a' organ she 'd learn her to play fer her board. So I thought I 'd tackle him ag'in, an' I was as cunnin' as I knowed how to be. I said how good Barb'ry was, an' how she could sing like a bird, an' how we 'd all enjoy music, an' it would n't cost much. But laws! I might as well talked to the wind. He sot that mouth o' hisn, an' says, says he, "My girls can play on the washboard; that 's the insterment their mother hed; an' I won't hev no finniky school-misses boardin' here, puttin' things in their heads. There 's a leetle more o' that now than I fancy."

46

That 's a hit at me, you see; but laws! I
did n't care. I guess I was too old to be in
love when I married, an' somehow he did n't
make me feel very sentimental, as they call
it. I sot out to do my duty, though, an' I
tried to do it. I tole Barb'ry it was no use
talkin' 'bout a' organ; an' she cried an' said,
"Ef pap was a pore man I would n't want it.
But he 's rich, an' he might let us be a little
like other folk; an', ma," she went on, "ef
my mother hed n't had sich a hard time I
believe she 'd ben a-livin' yet; but I guess
pap did n't mean it—I ought to be ashamed."
An' she wiped her eyes an' went up-stairs.
Well, things went on the same way. But I
was gettin' to think lots o' the children. The
boys was rough sometimes, but I allays liked
boys, an' never told tales; an' when Steve
wanted me to praise his colt,—fer his pap
he' d give him a fine one,—or Bob wanted
me to give his calf more 'n its share o' milk,
or little Tom wanted anything I could get fer
him, I allays humored 'em; an' I knew they
liked me, ef I was n't their own mother.

We had an awful lot o' work the summer

a year after I went there. He put in a big crop, fer he said he was bound to pay fer a twenty-acre pasture he hed jist bought, an' so we hed to be up airly an' late. You see, he got two more cows, an' hired another hand; an' I declare it was like a big hotel, only I believe it was harder. An' I thought he 'd work hisself to death, too, fer there was n't a lazy bone in his body; an' the boys —I was sorry fer the little fellers. It seems to me folks thinks children never gets tired. Why, I 've knowed Bob to be that wore out thet he 'd crawl up-stairs at night on his hands an' knees; but I could n't do nothin'— only be good to 'em.

Well, one day he fell out with the hand thet I 'd seen Em'ly liked, an' turned him off —right in harvest-time, too. An' thet didn't help matters, fer Em'ly sulked, an' the man was a good worker an' his place could n't be filled. An' so the squire was cross as a bear, an' him an' Em'ly had several fusses, an' at last she told him she was goin' to marry Sam White—thet was the feller's name. My! I 'll never forget thet time. But it 's no use talkin' it over. Em'ly faced her pap to the last, an' me an' Barb'ry cried; an' it ended in Em'ly packin' up her things an' goin' to one o' the neighbors. An' I must say I don't believe what came afterward would have happened if Em'ly had n't aggervated him the way she did.

Of course it was n't any easier on me an' Barb'ry after Em'ly was gone, though I do say the hired men was awful clever, helpin' us whenever they could; an' I says to Barb'ry one day, "Don't you fall in love with any one o' them boys, fer I can't spare you." An' she laughed, an' her face turned red; an' you could 'a' upsot me with a feather when she says, cried-like, "I won't, ma; I 'm engaged to Phil Thomas." "Barb'ry Hillyer," says I, "you ain't no such thing!" "Yes, I am, ma," she says; "but we 're goin' to wait till he 's of age; he 's only turned twenty now." "Dear me!" thinks I, "what will the squire say?" You see, I never 'd thought of Barb'ry carin' fer anybody. All the young fellers in the neighborhood took every chance to be with her, an' was comin' to the house on

HENRY McCARTER.

errands, or to see Steve, an' hangin' round
Sundays; but laws! I never thought o' her
carin' more fer one than t' other; an' I wondered how it would turn out. Phil was a
very nice boy, but his folks was n't very well
off, an' I felt worried. An' so time went on.
Harvest was over, an' Em'ly married, an' her
man, we heard, had rented a farm in the
neighborhood, when one day, Barb'ry an' me
bein' busy in the kitchen, the squire come
in, seemin' in a mighty good humor, an' he
says, "I tell you, mother,"—he called me
that nearly always,—"I 've had a streak of
luck. I got a big price for Selim, an' he 's
gone." Now Selim was the name Steve had
given his colt; an' I says, "Selim! Why, you
surely have n't sold Steve's colt?" He
laughed. "Steve's colt," he said, "but my
horse; the beast 's over four years old."
"O pap," said Barb'ry, "you ought n't done
it; Steve loved him so!" "I'll give him the
black colt," said pap, "an' a new suit o'
clothes; that 'll make it all right." But it
did n't. When Steve found his horse had
been sold he flew into a dreadful rage; an' I

could n't blame him, though I tried to pacify him, tellin' him his pap hed a right to do as he pleased. "He hed no right to sell my horse," cried the boy; "he gave him to me right at first, an' I raised him, an' he 'd nicker to me an' let me do anything with him, an' I loved him; an' fer pap to sell him, without even tellin' me, he 's no better than a horse-thief!"

"O Stevey," says I, "don't talk so; it 's wicked." But the boy was wild. "It 's not wicked to tell the truth," he said. "What 'd he give him to me fer, ef he was goin' to sell him? I say he is a thief to sell what did n't belong to him!" Oh dear, dear! His pap heerd Steve, fer jist then he came in, an' grabbed the boy by the collar, an' flung him across the room. The poor fellow staggered an' saved himself from fallin'; an' the squire caught him again, kicked him savagely, an', openin' the door, threw him into the yard. You need n't think Steve did n't show fight; but what could a slender lad of fifteen do against a strong man? I was that scared I could n't move or speak; an' as fer Barb'ry,

she was white as a sheet as her pap shut the
door on Steve and turned around. He looked
at us a minit; his eyes was glarin' an' his face
red as fire. "You git to work, miss; an' as
fer you," he said to me, "you let that boy
alone; none o' your pettin' him; do you hear?"
I did n't say a word, an' he went in the room,
bangin' the door to after him.

We looked at each other. Then Barb'ry,
with her white face set sort o' like her father's, walked to the kitchen door, opened
it, an' went out in the darkness; fer it was a
cloudy evening, an' supper was late, owin' to
the men bein' at work in the lower meadow.
I dished up the meal, an' called all hands;
but neither Barb'ry nor Steve came in, an' we
ate without 'em. I was mighty feared their
pap would ask for 'em, but he did n't; an' as
soon as the men went out o' the kitchen I
went to look fer 'em. I soon found Barb'ry;
she was settin' on the back porch, cryin'.
But she would n't say one thing about Steve.
She dried her eyes, an' helped do up the
work, an' then went up-stairs—said her head
ached an' she was goin' to bed. I had to go

in the room, as it was bed-time, an' I did n't know what to do. I slipped out, an' hunted for Steve. Then I went up-stairs, thinkin' mebbe he 'd gone round the house to the front door. But he had n't, an' the boys said they had n't saw him. So I had to say, before I lay down, "I guess Steve ain't in the house."

"Let him stay out, then," said the squire, angry as ever—he had n't spoke to me all the evenin' since the fuss. "I 'll let him know I 'm boss here."

1 did n't sleep much that night, an' I thought, "Well, Sally Humphrey was a happier woman than Mrs. Squire Hillyer, I reckon, but 'Mrs.' does sound better." Not a word was said in the mornin' till breakfast was called. Then little Tom asked fer Steve. "I reckon he 's asleep in the barn," said pap. "Go tell him to come in; he 's acted the fool long enough." The boy went, but soon came back, saying he "could n't find Steve." I see squire's face change color; but he sat down to the table without a word, an' we was about half through breakfast

when there was a knock at the back door. Barb'ry opened the door, an' a strange man walked in. "Squire," he said, "good mornin'. That horse I bought of yer yesterday is missin', an' I thought mebbe I 'd find him here. He either got out o' the stable or was taken out."

For a minit nobody spoke. Then Tommy said, "Pap, Selim ain't here. Mebbe Steve's gone after him."

"Who 's Steve?" said the stranger. "He is my son," answered pap, quickly. "You shall have our help, sir, in gettin' your horse. Set down an' eat a bite while I look about a bit." The stranger sat down, an' Barb'ry poured his coffee, while I followed the squire out. As soon as the door closed behind us he grabbed my arm. "Where 's that boy?" he whispered savagely. "I don't know," I said—fer I did n't. He looked at me; his face turned 'most the color of ashes. "O God!" he cried; then he hurried toward the stable.

I was kind o' stunned fer a while. I saw he thought Steve had gone an' got the horse, an' was gone. But I knew better. I felt somehow Steve was not that kind of a boy. The stranger came out, an' pretty soon he an' the squire rode off. I went in to Barb'ry. She was tryin' to eat, with tears runnin' down her face.

"Barb'ry," said I, "where kin Steve be? Your pap's nearly crazy fer fear he has stole' Selim an' gone off." Barb'ry's face flamed up. "Steve's no thief," she said, "wherever he is"; an' I could n't get another word out o' her. It was an awful long, hot day, an' we had a big ironin' to do. Barb'ry worked hard all mornin', but after dinner she got real sick, an' I made her go out o' doors an' set in the shade. After a while I heerd her call me, an' goin' out, I see Phil Thomas a-talkin' to her.

"Ma," she called out, as soon as she see me, "Phil says Steve's at their house, an' has been all night. I thought he'd go there or to Em'ly's." "Is he comin' home?" I asked Phil. He shook his head. "Em'ly is at our house now," he said, "an' I think he'll go home with her. He is pretty badly hurt from a fall, he says, an' is somewhat lame; but he 'll get along." I went in to my ironin', feelin' thankful, an' left the youngsters to themselves. Bless 'em! they made a pretty pair.

Phil stayed till about four o'clock, an' after he was gone Barb'ry come in to help about supper. "I wish pap 'd come," she kep' sayin'; "I want him to know Steve is no thief." Presently she ran out on the back porch, an' stood lookin' down the road, an' I heerd the clatterin' of a horse; an' I run out jist in time to see Barb'ry go like a flash out of the back gate toward the stable. It was all over in a minit. I see the horse r'ar up as she flung the open door to; I see her pap hangin' with one foot in the stirrup, his head draggin', though one hand still held the bridle; an' I got to him somehow jist as he got his foot loose, an' I helped him up; an' there lay Barb'ry white an' still. Her pap let go the horse, an' stooped down. "Barb'ry!" he said. She never moved. "She 's dead," I said; "what done it? O Barb'ry, my precious, what hurt you?" "Be still!"

he said sharply; "she's not dead. Help get
her in the house." We lifted her up, an'
she opened her eyes. "Phil," she whispered
faintly, "tell pap Steve—" then her voice
ceased, an' her sweet eyes shut again. We
got her on the bed, an' I got the camphire,
an' pap rung the big bell fer the hands, an'
soon as they come in sent one fer the doctor.
But I found where she was hurt; there was
a great ugly bruise right between her pretty
white shoulders. A little stream o' blood
begun to trickle out o' her mouth. "Send
over to Thomas's," I said, "for Phil an' Steve
an' Em'ly." He thought I 'd lost my senses,
I know. "They 're there," I said; "Phil was
here." In spite o' his trouble his face lighted
up. "Then Steve is not—" he began; but
at the name Barb'ry's eyes opened again.
"Never mind pap; he don't—he don't mean
it, Stevey," she muttered. "I know it 's
hard, but I guess he likes us children." "Go,"
I said, "send fer 'em." He went out, with
that queer gray color creepin' over his face
that I see in the mornin'. An' pretty soon
I heerd the horse gallopin' off. Then he

come back. Well, we done all we could.
The doctor came, an' Phil an' Steve an' Em'ly
an' her man. But she never spoke but once
after they came. She murmured then bro-
kenly; all we could make out was, "Pap—Steve
never—ma's real good—Phil— Mother!"
she cried aloud at last, an' her eyes opened
wide, an' she looked wonderingly at us, fixin'
her gaze fer a little on her pap, who stood at
the foot of the bed. Then a long shudder
shook her body, an' her breath came in gasps;
a torrent of blood poured out o' her mouth,
an' she was gone.

Yes, we had to bear it. People can bear
things when they have to. But he's never
been the same man, an' his face keeps that
queer color. I've heerd that when that
ashy look comes to anybody they've got
their death-blow; they may live a few years,
but it's death it means.

"How did he get throwed?" Well, you
see, jist as he rode in at the barn-yard gate
the horse sheered an' throwed him, an' his
feet caught. Barb'ry see it all, an' see the

stable-door open. She knowed the horse 'd
make fer his stall, an' her pap's brains 'd be
knocked out; an' she got there in time to
shut the door, an' when the horse r'ard up
he struck her afore she could git out o' the

way. Yes, Steve stayed at home; I dunno
what we 'd do without him. An' Em'ly an'
her man comes over right often. She has a
little girl now. She calls it Barb'ry, an' it 's
mighty cute; but it 'll never be like my Bar-
b'ry to me, or pap either. An', after all,

Selim had got out himself, an' was on his way home when they caught him. But pore Stevey, he said he never wanted to see him again.

Phil Thomas? He was pretty downhearted fer a good while; but he 's chirked up now, an' I heerd he was waitin' on Melinda Jones. She 's a nice girl, but she could n't hold a candle to Barb'ry.

"Dead folks soon forgot," you say? I don't believe it. Folks don't forget, but they can't go mournin' always. An' it would n't be right ef they could. I know, long as I live, I 'll never forgit my girlie, who give up her sweet young life to save her pap. No; I 'm not sorry I married him either. He 's awful good, ef he is a little close with money. But that 's his nature. I reckon it 's 'cause he knows how hard it is to git. But bless my heart! it 's nigh four o'clock, and that girl will never git supper on without I see to it, so you must excuse me awhile. There 's the album with Barb'ry's picter in it. 'T ain't half as pretty as she was, but you can guess a little what she 's like by it.

Ef you see him comin' jist slip it out o' sight; he can't bear to see it. There's some o' my folks' likenesses in it, too. No; I never did hev mine taken. Don't reckon I ever will. But laws! I must see about supper.

THE HOME-COMING OF COLONEL HUCKS

BY

WILLIAM ALLEN WHITE

THE HOME-COMING OF
COLONEL HUCKS

❧

A GENERATION ago, a wagon covered
with white canvas turned to the right
on the California road, and took a northerly
course toward the prairie stream that nestled
just under a long, low bluff. When the white
pilgrim, jolting over the rough, unbroken
ground through the tall "blue-stem" grass,
reached a broad bend in the stream, it
stopped. A man and a woman emerged from
under the canvas, and stood for a moment
facing the wild green meadow and the distant hills. The man was young, lithe, and
graceful, and, despite his boyish figure, the
woman felt his unconscious strength as he

put his arm about her waist. She was aglow with health. Her fine, strong, intelligent eyes burned with hope, and her firm jaw was good to behold. They stood gazing at the virgin field a moment, in silence. There were tears in the woman's eyes as she looked up after the kiss, and said:

"And this is the end of our wedding-journey; and—and—the honeymoon, the only one we can ever have in all the world, is over."

The horses, moving uneasily in their sweaty harness, cut short the man's reply.

When he returned, his wife was getting the cooking-utensils from under the wagon, and life—stern, troublous—had begun for them.

It was thus that young Colonel William Hucks brought his wife to Kansas.

They were young, strong, hearty people, and they conquered the wilderness. A home sprang up in the elbow of the stream. In the fall long rows of corn-shucks trailed what had been the meadow. In the summer the field stood horse-high with corn. From

the bluff, as the years flew by, the spectator
might see the checker-board of the farm,
clean cut, well kept, smiling in the sun.
Little children frolicked in the king row, and
hurried to school down the green lines of the
lanes where the hedges grow. Once a slow
procession, headed by a spring wagon with
a little black box in it, might have been seen
filing between the rows of the half-grown
poplar-trees, and out across the brown stub-
ble-covered prairie, to the desolate hill and
the graveyard. Now neighbors from miles
around may be heard coming in the rattling
wagons across vale and plain, laden with tin
presents; after which the little home is seen
ablaze with lights, while the fiddle vies with
the mirth of the frolicking party, dancing
with the wanton echoes on the bluff across
the stream.

There were years when the light in the
kitchen burned far into the night, when two
heads bent over the table, figuring to make
ends meet. In these years the girlish figure
became bent and the light faded in the
woman's eyes, while the lithe figure of the

man was gnarled by the rigors of the struggle.

There were days—not years, thank God— when lips forgot their tenderness; and as fate tugged fiercely at the curbed bit, there were times when souls rebelled and cried out in bitterness and despair at the roughness of the path. In this wise went Colonel Hucks and his wife through youth into maturity, and in this wise they faced toward the sunset.

He was tall, with a stoop, grizzled, brawny, perhaps uncouth in mien. She was stout, unshapely, rugged; yet her face was kind and motherly. There was a boyish twinkle left in her husband's eyes, and a quaint, quizzing, one-sided smile often stumbled across his care-furrowed countenance. As the years passed, Mrs. Hucks noticed that her husband's foot fell heavily when he walked by her side, and the pang she felt when she first observed his plodding step was too deep for tears. It was in these days that the minds of the Huckses unconsciously reverted to old times. It became their wont, in these latter days, to sit in the silent house whence the children had gone out to try issue with the world, and of evenings to talk of the old faces and of the old places in the home of their youth. Theirs had been a pinched and busy life. They had never returned to visit their old Ohio home. The colonel's father and mother were gone. His wife's relatives were not there. Yet each felt the longing to go back. For years they had talked of the charms of the home of their childhood. Their children had been brought up to believe that the place was little less than heaven. The Kansas grass seemed short and barren of beauty to them beside the picture of the luxury of Ohio's fields. For them the Kansas streams did not ripple and dimple so merrily in the sun as the Ohio brooks that romped through the dewy pastures in their memories. The bleak Kansas plain in winter and in fall seemed to the colonel and his wife to be ugly and gaunt when they remembered the brow of the hill under which their first kiss was shaded from the moon, while the world grew dim under a sleigh that bounded over the turnpike. The old people did not give

71

voice to their musings, but in the woman's heart there gnawed a yearning for the beauty of the old scenes. It was almost a physical hunger.

After their last child, a girl, had married and had gone down the lane toward the lights of the village, Mrs. Hucks began to watch with a greedy eye the dollars mount toward a substantial bank-account. She hoped that she and her husband might afford a holiday.

Last year Providence had blessed the Huckses with plenty. It was the woman who revived the friendship of youth in her husband's cousin, who lived in the old township in Ohio. It was Mrs. Hucks who secured from that cousin an invitation to spend a few weeks in the Ohio homestead. It was Mrs. Hucks, again, who made her husband happy by putting him into a tailor's suit—the first he had bought since his wedding—for the great occasion. Colonel Hucks needed no persuasion to take the trip. Indeed, it was his wife's economy which had kept him from being a spendthrift, and from borrowing money with which to go on a dozen different occasions.

The day which Colonel and Mrs. William Hucks set apart for starting upon their journey was one of those perfect Kansas days in early October. The rain had washed the summer's dust from the air, clearing it, and stenciling the lights and shades very sharply. The woods along the little stream which flowed through the farm had not been greener at any time through the season. The second crop of grass on the hillside almost sheened in vividness. The yellow of the stubble in the grain-fields was all but a glittering golden. The sky was a deep, glorious blue, and the big, downy clouds which lumbered lazily here and there in the depths of it appeared near and palpable.

As Mrs. Hucks "did up" the breakfast dishes for the last time before leaving for the town to take the cars, she began to feel that the old house would be lonesome without her. The silence that was about to come seemed to her to be seeping in, and it made her feel "creepy." In her fancy she petted

the furniture as she "set it to rights," saying mentally that it would be a long time
before the house would have her care again.
To Mrs. Hucks every bit of furniture brought
up its separate recollection, and there was a
hatchet-scarred chair in the kitchen which
had come with her in the wagon from Ohio.
Mrs. Hucks felt that she could not leave that
chair.   All the while she was singing softly
as she went about her simple tasks.   Her
husband was puttering around the barn-yard,
with the dog under his feet.   He was re-
peating for the twentieth time the instruc-
tions to a neighbor about the care of the
stock, when it occurred to him to go into the
house and dress.   After this was accom-
plished, the old couple paused outside the
front door, while Colonel Hucks fumbled with
the key.

"Think of it, father," said Mrs. Hucks, as
she turned to descend from the porch.
"Thirty years ago—and you and I have been
fighting so hard out here—since you let me
out of your arms while you went to look after
the horses.   Think of what has come—and

—and—gone, father, and here we are alone after it all."

"Now, mother, I—" But the woman broke in again with:

"Do you mind how I looked that day? Oh, William, you were so fine and so handsome then. What's become of my boy—my young, sweet, strong, glorious boy?"

Mrs. Hucks's eyes were wet, and her voice broke at the end of the sentence.

"Mother," said the colonel, as he went around the corner of the house, "just wait a minute till I see if the kitchen door is fastened."

When he came back, he screwed up the corner of his mouth into a droll, one-sided smile, and, with a twinkle in his eyes, said to the woman emerging from her handkerchief:

"Mother, for a woman of your age, I should say you had a mighty close call to being kissed just then. That kitchen door was all that saved you."

"Now, pa, don't be silly," was all that Mrs. Hucks had the courage to attempt, as she climbed into the buggy.

Colonel Hucks and his wife went down the road, each loath to go and leave the place without their care. Their ragged, uneven flow of talk was filled with more anxiety about the place which they were leaving than it was with the joys anticipated at their journey's end. The glories of Ohio, and the wonderful green of its hills, and the cool of its meadows veined with purling brooks, was a picture that seemed to fade in the mental vision of this old pair when they turned the corner that hid their old Kansas home from view. Mrs. Hucks kept reverting in her mind to her recollection of the bedroom which she had left in disorder. The parlor and the kitchen formed a mental picture, in the housewife's fancy, which did not leave space for speculations about the glories into which she was about to come. In the cars, Colonel Hucks found himself leaning across the aisle, bragging mildly about Kansas, for the benefit of a traveling man from Cincinnati. When the colonel and his wife spread their supper on their knees in the Kansas City Union Depot, the recollection that it was the little buff Cochin pullet which they were eating made Mrs. Hucks very homesick. The colonel, on being reminded of this, was meditative also.

They arrived at their destination in the night. Mrs. Hucks and the women of the homestead refreshed old acquaintance in the bedroom and in the kitchen, while the colonel and the men sat stiffly in the parlor and called the roll of the dead and the absent. In the morning, while he was waiting for his breakfast, Colonel Hucks went for a prowl down in the cow-lot. It seemed to him that the creek which ran through the lot was dry and ugly. He found a stone upon which, as a boy, he had stood and fished. He remembered it as a huge boulder, and he had told his children wonderful tales about its great size. It seemed to him that it had worn away one half in thirty years. The moss on the river-bank was faded and old, and the beauty for which he had looked was marred by a thousand irregularities which he did not recall in the picture of the place that he had carried in his memory since he left it.

Colonel Hucks trudged up the bank from the stream with his hands clasped behind him, whistling "O Lord, remember me," and trying to reconcile the things he had seen with those he had expected to find. At breakfast he said nothing of his puzzle; but as Mrs. Hucks and the colonel sat in the parlor alone, during the morning, while their cousins were arranging to take the Kansas people over the neighborhood in the buggy, Mrs. Hucks said:

"Father, I have been looking out the window, and I see they 've had such a dreadful drought here. See that grass there; it 's as short and dry; and the ground looks burneder and crackeder than it does in Kansas."

"Uhm, yes," replied the colonel. "I had noticed that myself. Yet the crops seem a pretty fair yield this year."

As the buggy in which the two families were riding rumbled over the bridge, the colonel, who was sitting in the front seat, turned to the woman in the back seat, and said:

"Lookie there, mother; they've got a new mill—smaller 'n the old mill, too." To which his cousin responded, "Bill Hucks, what's got into you, anyway? That's the same old mill where me and you used to steal pigeons."

The colonel looked closer, and drawled out, "Well, I be dog-goned! What makes it look so small? Ain't it smaller, mother?" he asked, as they crossed the mill-race, that seemed to the colonel to be a diminutive affair compared with the roaring mill-race in which, as a boy, he had caught minnows.

The party rode on thus for half an hour, chatting leisurely, when Mrs. Hucks, who had been keenly watching the scenery for five minutes, pinched her husband, and cried enthusiastically, as the buggy was descending a little knoll:

"Here 't is, father. This is the place."

"What place?" asked the colonel, who was head over heels in the tariff.

"Don't you know, William?" replied his

wife, with a tremble in her voice which the woman beside her noticed.

Every one in the buggy was listening. The colonel looked about him; then, turning to the woman beside his wife in the back seat, he said:

"This is the place where I mighty nigh got tipped over trying to drive two horses to a sleigh with lines between my knees. Mother and me have remembered it, some way, ever since."

And the old man stroked his grizzled beard, and tried to smile on the wrong side of his face, that the women might see his joke. They exchanged meaning glances when the colonel turned away, and Mrs. Hucks was proudly happy. Even the dullness of the color on the grass, which she had remembered as luscious green, did not sadden her for half an hour.

When the two Kansas people were alone that night, the colonel asked:

"Don't it seem kind of dwarfed here to what you expected it would be ? Seems to me like it 's all shriveled, and worn out, and old. Everything 's got dust on it. The grass by the road is dusty. The trees that used to seem so tall and black with shade are just nothing like what they used to be. The hill I 've thought of as a young mountain don't seem to be so big as our bluff back— back home."

Kansas was home to them now. For thirty years the struggling couple on the prairie had kept the phrase " back home " sacred to Ohio. Each felt a thrill at the household blasphemy, and both were glad that the colonel had said "back home," and that it meant Kansas.

"Are you sorry you came, father?" said Mrs. Hucks, as the colonel was about to fall into a doze.

"I don't know; are you ?" he asked.

"Well, yes; I guess I am. I have n't no heart for this, the way it is, and I 've someway lost the picture I had fixed in my mind of the way it was. I don't care for this, and yet it seems like I do, too. Oh, I wish I hadn't come, to find everything so washed out like it is."

And so they looked at pictures of youth through the eyes of age. How the colors were faded! What a tragic difference there is between the light which springs from the dawn, and the glow which falls from the sunset!

After the first day Colonel Hucks did not restrain his bragging about Kansas; and Mrs. Hucks gave rein to her pride when she heard him. Before that day she had reserved a secret contempt for the Kansas boaster, and had ever wished that he might see what Ohio could do in the particular line which he was praising. But now Mrs. Hucks caught herself saying to her hostess, "What small ears of corn you raise here!"

The day after this concession Mrs. Hucks began to grow homesick At first she worried about the stock; the colonel's chief care was about the dog. The fifth day's visit was their last. As they were driving to the town to take the train for Kansas, Mrs. Hucks heard her husband discoursing something after this fashion:

"I tell you, Jim, before I 'd slave my life

out on an 'eighty' the way you 're doin', I 'd go out takin' in whitewashin'. It is just like this: a man in Kansas has lower taxes, better schools, and more advantages in every way, than you 've got here. And as for grass-hoppers! Why, Jim West, sech talk makes me tired. My boy Bill 's been always born and raised in Kansas, and now he 's in the legislature; and in all his life, since he can remember, he never seen a hopper; would n't know one from a sacred ibex, if he met it in the road."

While the women were sitting in the buggy at the depot waiting for the train, Mrs. Hucks found herself saying:

"And as for fruit—why, we fed apples to the hogs this fall. I sold the cherries, all but what was on one tree near the house, and I put up sixteen quarts from just two sides of that tree, and never stepped my foot off the ground to pick 'em."

When they were comfortably seated on the homeward-bound train, Mrs. Hucks said to her husband:

"How do you suppose they live here in

this country, anyway, father? Don't any one here seem to own any of the land join-in' them, and they 'd no more think of put-tin' in water-tanks and windmills around their farms than they 'd think of flyin'. I just wish Mary could come out and see my new kitchen sink with the hot and cold water in it. Why, she almost fainted when I told her how to fix a dreen for her dish-water and things." Then, after a sigh, she added, "But they are so onprogressive here nowadays."

That was the music which the colonel loved, and he took up the strain, and carried the tune for a few miles. Then it became a duet, and the two old souls were very happy.

They were overjoyed at being bound for Kansas; they hungered for kindred spirits. At Peoria, in the early morning, they awakened from their chair-car naps to hear a strident female voice saying:

"Well, sir, when the raid did finally come, Mr. Morris he just did n't think there was a thing left worth cutting on the place, but, lo and behold, we got over forty bushel to the acre off of that field as it was."

The colonel was thoroughly awake in an instant, and he nudged his wife as the voice went on:

"Mr. Morris he was so afraid the wheat was winter-killed; all the papers said it was; and then came the late frost, which every one said had ruined it; but law me!"

Mrs. Hucks could stand it no longer. With her husband's cane she reached the owner of the voice, and said:

"Excuse me, ma'am, but what part of Kansas are you from?"

It seemed like meeting a dear relative. The rest of the journey to Kansas City was a halleluiah chorus, wherein the colonel sang a powerful and telling bass.

When he crossed the Kansas State line, Colonel Hucks began indeed to glory in his State. He pointed out the school-houses that rose in every village, and asked his fellow-passenger to note that the school-house is the most important piece of architecture in every group of buildings. He told the

history of every rod of ground along the
Kaw to Topeka. He dilated eloquently and
at length upon the coal-mines in Osage
County, and he pointed with pride to the
varied resources of his State. Every pros-
pect was pleasing to Colonel Hucks as he
rode home that beautiful day, and his wife
was more radiantly happy than she had been
for many years.

As the train pulled into the little town of
Willow Creek that afternoon, the colonel
craned his head at the car window to catch
the first glimpse of the big red stand-pipe,
and of the big stone school-house on the hill.
When the whistle blew for the station, the
colonel said:

"What is it that fool Riley feller says
about 'Grigsby's Station, where we used to
be so happy and so pore'?"

As the colonel and his wife passed out of
the town into the quiet country, where the
shadows were growing long and black, and
where the gentle blue haze was hanging over
the distant hills that undulated the horizon,
a silence fell upon the two hearts. Each

mind sped back over a lifetime to the evening when they had turned out of the main road in which they were traveling. A dog barking in the meadow behind the hedge did not startle them from their reveries. The restless cattle wandering down the hillside toward the bars made a natural complement to the picture which they loved.

"It is almost sunset, father," said the wife, as she put her hand on her husband's arm.

Her touch, and the voice in which she had spoken, tightened some cord at his throat. The colonel could only repeat, as he avoided her gaze:

"Yes, almost sunset, mother—almost sunset."

"It has been a long day, William, but you have been good to me. Has it been a happy day for you, father?"

The colonel turned his head away. He was afraid to trust himself to speech. He clucked to the horses, and drove down the lane. As they came into the yard, the colonel put an arm about his wife, and pressed his cheek against her face. Then he said drolly:

"Now lookie at that dog come tearin' up here like he never saw white folks before."

And so Colonel William Hucks brought his wife back to Kansas. Here their youth is woven into the very soil they love; here every tree around their home has its sacred history; here every sky above them recalls some day of trial and hope.

Here in the gloaming to-night stands an old man, bent and grizzled. His eyes are dimmed with tears which he would not acknowledge for the world, and he is dreaming strange dreams, while he listens to a little cracked voice in the kitchen half humming and half singing:

> "Home again, home again,
> From a foreign shore."

A POINT OF KNUCKLIN' DOWN

BY

ELLA HIGGINSON

A POINT OF KNUCKLIN' DOWN

❧

IT was the day before Christmas—an Oregon Christmas. It had rained mistily at dawn, but at ten o'clock the clouds had parted and moved away reluctantly. There was a blue and dazzling sky overhead. The raindrops still sparkled on the windows and on the green grass, and the last roses and chrysanthemums hung their beautiful heads heavily beneath them; but there was to be no more rain. Oregon City's mighty barometer—the Falls of the Willamette—was declaring to her people, by her softened roar, that the morrow was to be fair.

Mrs. Orville Palmer was in the large kitchen, making preparations for the Christmas dinner. She was a picture of dainty loveliness in a lavender gingham dress, made with a full skirt and a shirred waist and big leg-o'-mutton sleeves. A white apron was tied neatly around her waist.

Her husband came in, and paused to put his arm around her and kiss her. She was stirring something on the stove, holding her dress aside with one hand.

"It 's goin' to be a fine Christmas, Emarine," he said, and sighed unconsciously. There was a wistful and care-worn look on his face.

"Beautiful!" said Emarine, vivaciously. "Goin' down-town, Orville?"

"Yes. Want anything?"

"Why, the cranberries ain't come yet. I 'm so uneasy about 'em. They 'd ought to 'a' be'n stooed long ago. I like 'em cooked down an' strained to a jell. I don't see what ails them groc'rymen. Sh'u'd think they c'u'd get around sometime before doomsday! Then I want—here, you 'd best set it down." She took a pencil and a slip of paper from a shelf over the table, and

gave them to him. "Now, let me see." She
commenced stirring again, with two little
wrinkles between her brows. "A ha'f a
pound o' citron, a ha'f a pound o' candied
peel, two pounds o' cur'nts, two pounds o'
raisins,—get 'em stunned, Orville,—a pound
o' sooet,—make 'em give you some that ain't
all strings,—a box o' Norther' Spy apples, a
ha'f a dozen lemons, four bits' worth o' wal-
nuts or a'monds, whichever 's freshest, a pint
o' Puget Sound oysters fer the dressin', an'
a bunch o' cel'ry. You stop by an' see about
the turkey, Orville; an' I wish you 'd run in 's
you go by mother's, an' tell her to come up
as soon as she can. She 'd ought to be here
now."

Her husband smiled as he finished the list.
"You 're a wonderful housekeeper, Emarine,"
he said.

Then his face grew grave. "Got a present
for your mother yet, Emarine?"

"Oh, yes, long ago. I got her a black
shawl down t' Charman's. She 's be'n
wantin' one."

He shuffled his feet about a little. "Unh-hunh. You—that is—I reckon you ain't picked out any present fer—fer my mother, have you, Emarine?"

"No," she replied with cold distinctness, "I ain't."

There was a silence. Emarine stirred briskly. The lines grew deeper between her brows. Two red spots came into her cheeks. "I hope the rain ain't spoilt the chrysyanthums," she said then, with an air of ridding herself of a disagreeable subject.

Orville made no answer. He moved his feet again uneasily. Presently he said: "I expect my mother needs a black shawl, too. Seemed to me hern looked kind o' rusty at church Sunday. Notice it, Emarine?"

"No," said Emarine.

"Seemed to me she was gittin' to look offul old. Emarine"—his voice broke; he came a step nearer—"it 'll be the first Christmas dinner I ever eat without my mother."

She drew back, and looked at him. He knew the look that flashed into her eyes, and shrank from it.

" You don't have to eat this 'n' without her, Orville Parmer! You go an' eat your dinner with your mother 'f you want! I can get along alone. Are you goin' to order them things? If you ain't, just say so, an' I'll go an' do 't myself!"

He put on his hat and went without a word.

Mrs. Palmer took the saucepan from the stove, and set it on the hearth. Then she sat down, and leaned her cheek in the palm of her hand, and looked steadily out the window. Her eyelids trembled closer together. Her eyes held a far-sighted look. She saw a picture, but it was not the picture of the blue reaches of sky and the green valley cleft by its silver-blue river. She saw a kitchen, shabby compared to her own, scantily furnished, and in it an old white-haired woman sitting down to eat her Christmas dinner alone.

After a while she arose with an impatient sigh. "Well, I can't help it!" she exclaimed. "If I knuckled down to her this time I'd have to do 't ag'in. She might just as well get ust to 't first as last. I wish she had n't got to lookin' so old an' pitiful, though, a-settin' there in front o' us in church Sunday after Sunday. The cords stand out in her neck like well-rope, an' her chin keeps a-quiv'rin' so! I can see Orville a-watchin' her—"

The door opened suddenly, and her mother entered. She was bristling with curiosity. "Say, Emarine!" She lowered her voice, although there was no one to hear. "Where d' you s'pose the undertaker 's a-goin' up by here? Have you hear of anybody—"

"No," said Emarine. "Did Orville stop by an' tell you to hurry up?"

"Yes. What 's the matter of him? Is he sick?"

"Not as I know of. Why?"

"He looks so. Oh, I wonder if it 's one o' the Peterson children where the undertaker 's a-goin'! They 've all got the quinsy sore throat."

"How does he look? I don't see 's he looks so turrable."

"Why, Emarine Parmer! Ev'rybody in

town says he looks *so!* I only hope they don't know what ails him!"

"What *does* ail him?" cried out Emarine, fiercely. "What are you hintin' at?"

"Well, if you don't know what ails him, you 'd ought to; so I 'll tell you. He 's dyin' by inches ever sence you turned his mother out o' doors."

Emarine turned white. Sheet-lightning played in her eyes.

"Oh, you 'd ought to talk about my turnin' her out!" she burst out furiously. "After you a-settin' here a-quar'l'n' with her in this very kitchen, an' eggin' me on! Wa'n't she goin' to turn you out o' your own daughter's home? Wa'n't that what I turned her out fer? I did n't turn her out, anyhow! I only told Orville this house wa'n't big enough fer his mother an' me, an' that neither o' us 'u'd knuckle down, so he 'd best take his choice. You 'd ought to talk!"

"Well, if I egged you on I 'm sorry fer 't," said Mrs. Endey, solemnly. "Ever sence that fit o' sickness I had a month ago, I 've felt kind o' old an' no-account myself, as if

I 'd like to let all holts go an' jest rest. I
don't spunk up like I ust to. No, he did n't
go to Peterson's—he 's gawn right on. My
land! I wonder 'f it ain't old Gran'ma Eliot;
she had a bad spell—no, he did n't turn that
corner. I can't think where he 's goin' to!"

She sat down with a sigh of defeat.

A smile glimmered palely across Emarine's
face, and was gone. "Maybe if you 'd go
up in the antic you could see better," she
suggested dryly.

"Oh, Emarine, here comes old Gran'ma
Eliot herself! Run an' open the door fer her.
She 's limpin' worse 'n usual."

Emarine flew to the door. Grandma Eliot
was one of the few people she loved. She
was large and motherly. She wore a black
dress and shawl, and a funny bonnet with a
frill of white lace around her brow.

Emarine's face softened when she kissed
her. "I 'm so glad to see you," she said, and
her voice was tender.

Even Mrs. Endey's face underwent a
change. Usually it wore a look of doubt, if
not of positive suspicion, but now it fairly

beamed. She shook hands cordially with the guest, and led her to a comfortable chair.

"I know your rheumatiz is worse," she said cheerfully, "because you 're limpin' so. Oh, did you see the undertaker go up by here? We can't think where he 's goin' to. D' you happen to know?"

"No, I don't, an' I don't want to, neither." Mrs. Eliot laughed comfortably. "Mis' Endey, you don't ketch me foolin' with undertakers till I have to." She sat down, and removed her black cotton gloves. "I 'm gettin' to that age when I don't care much where undertakers go to so long 's they let *me* alone. Fixin' fer Christmas dinner, Emarine, dear?"

"Yes, ma'am," said Emarine in her very gentlest tone. Her mother had never said "dear" to her, and the sound of it on this old lady's lips was sweet. "Won't you come an' take dinner with us?" .

The old lady laughed merrily. "Oh, dearie me, dearie me! You don't guess my son's folks could spare me now, do you? I spend ev'ry Christmas there. They most carry me on two chips. My son's wife, Sidonie, she nearly runs her feet off waitin' on me. She can't do enough fer me. My! Mrs. Endey, you don't know what a comfort a daughter-in-law is when you get old an' feeble!"

Emarine's face turned red. She went to the table, and stood with her back to the older women; but her mother's sharp eyes observed that her ears grew scarlet.

"An' I never will," said Mrs. Endey, grimly.

"You've got a son-in-law, though, who's worth a whole townful of most sons-in-law. He was such a good son, too; jest worshiped his mother; could n't bear her out o' his sight. He humored her high and low. That's jest the way Sidonie does with me. I'm gettin' cranky 's I get older, an' sometimes I'm reel cross an' sassy to her; but she jest laffs at me, an' then comes an' kisses me, an' I'm all right again. It's a blessin' right from God to have a daughter-in-law like that."

The knife in Emarine's hand slipped, and she uttered a little cry.

"Hurt you?" demanded her mother, sternly.

Emarine was silent, and did not turn.

"Cut you, Emarine? Why don't you answer me? Aigh?"

"A little," said Emarine. She went into the pantry, and presently returned with a narrow strip of muslin, which she wound around her finger.

"Well, I never see! You never will learn any gumption! Why don't you look what you 're about? Now go around Christmas with your finger all tied up!"

"Oh, that 'll be all right by to-morrow," said Mrs. Eliot, cheerfully. "Won't it, Emarine? Never cry over spilt milk, Mrs. Endey; it makes a body get wrinkles too fast. O' course, Orville's mother 's comin' to take dinner with you, Emarine?"

"Dear me!" exclaimed Emarine, in a sudden flutter, "I don't see why them cranberries don't come! I told Orville to hurry 'em up. I 'd best make the floatin' island while I wait."

"I stopped at Orville's mother's as I come along, Emarine."

"How?" Emarine turned in a startled way from the table.

"I say I stopped at Orville's mother's as I come along."

"Oh!"

"She well?" asked Mrs. Endey.

"No, she ain't; shakin' like she had the St. Vitus' dance. She's failed harrable lately. She'd be'n cryin'; her eyes was all swelled up."

There was quite a silence. Then Mrs. Endey said, "What she be'n cryin' about?"

"Why, when I asked her she jest laffed kind o' pitiful, an' said, 'Oh, only my tomfoolishness, o' course.' Said she always got to thinkin' about other Christmases. But I cheered her up. I told her what a good time I always had at my son's, an' how Sidonie jest could n't do enough fer me. An' I told her to think what a nice time she'd have here 't Emarine's to-morrow."

Mrs. Endey smiled. "What she say to that?"

"She did n't say much. I could see she was thankful, though, she had a son's to go to. She said she pitied all poor wretches that had to set out their Christmas alone. Poor old lady! she ain't got much spunk left. She's all broke down. But I cheered her up some. Sech a *wishful* look took holt o' her when I pictchered her dinner over here at Emarine's. I can't seem to forget it. Goodness! I must go. I 'm on my way to Sidonie's, an' she 'll be comin' after me if I ain't on time."

When Mrs. Eliot had gone limping down the path, Mrs. Endey said, "You got your front room red up, Emarine?"

"No; I ain't had time to red up anything."

"Well, I 'll do it. Where 's your duster at?"

"Behind the org'n. You can get out the wax cross again. Mis' Dillon was here with all her childern, an' I had to hide up ev'rything. I never see childern like hern. She lets 'em handle things so!"

Mrs. Endey went into the "front room," and began to dust the organ. She was something of a diplomat, and she wished to be alone for a few minutes. "You have to manage Emarine by contrairies," she reflected. It did not occur to her that this was a family trait. "I'm offul sorry I ever egged her on to turnin' Orville's mother out o' doors, but who'd 'a' thought it 'u'd break her down so? She ain't told a soul, either. I reckoned she'd talk somethin' offul about us, but she ain't told a soul. She's kep' a stiff upper lip, an' told folks she al'ays expected to live alone when Orville got married. Emarine's all worked up. I believe the Lord Hisself must 'a' sent Gran'ma Eliot here to talk like an angel unawares. I bet she'd go an' ask Mis' Parmer over here to dinner if she wa'n't afraid I'd laff at her fer knucklin' down. I'll have to aggravate her."

She finished dusting, and returned to the kitchen. "I wonder what Gran'ma Eliot 'u'd say if she knew you'd turned Orville's mother out, Emarine?"

There was no reply. Emarine was at the table making tarts. Her back was to her mother.

"I did n't mean what I said about bein' sorry I egged you on, Emarine. I'm glad you turned her out. She 'd *ort* to be turned out."

Emarine dropped a quivering ruby of jelly into a golden ring of pastry, and laid it carefully on a plate.

"Gran'ma Eliot can go talkin' about her daughter-in-law Sidonie all she wants, Emarine. You keep a stiff upper lip."

"I can 'tend to my own affairs," said Emarine, fiercely.

"Well, don't flare up so. Here comes Orville. Land, but he does look peakid!"

After supper, when her mother had gone home for the night, Emarine put on her hat and shawl.

Her husband was sitting by the fireplace, looking thoughtfully at the bed of coals.

"I 'm goin' out," she said briefly. "You keep the fire up."

"Why, Emarine, it 's dark. Don't you want I sh'u'd go along?"

"No; you keep the fire up."

He looked at her anxiously, but he knew

from the way she set her heels down that remonstrance would be useless.

"Don't stay long," he said in a tone of habitual tenderness. He loved her passionately, in spite of the lasting hurt she had given him when she parted him from his mother. It was a hurt that had sunk deeper than even he realized. It lay heavy on his heart day and night. It took the blue out of the sky, and the green out of the grass, and the gold out of the sunlight. It took the exaltation and the rapture out of his tenderest moments of love.

He never reproached her, he never really blamed her; certainly he never pitied himself. But he carried a heavy heart around with him, and his few smiles were joyless things.

For the trouble, he blamed only himself. He had promised Emarine solemnly before he married her that if there were any "knuckling down" to be done, his mother should be the one to do it. He had made the promise deliberately, and he could no more have broken it than he could have changed the color of his eyes. When bitter feeling arises between two relatives by marriage, it is the one who stands between them—the one who is bound by the tenderest ties to both—who has the real suffering to bear, who is torn and tortured until life holds nothing worth the having. Orville Palmer was the one who stood between. He had built his own cross, and he took it up and bore it without a word.

Emarine hurried through the early winter dark until she came to the small and poor house where her husband's mother lived. It was off the main-traveled street.

There was a dim light in the kitchen; the curtain had not been drawn. Emarine paused, and looked in. The sash was lifted six inches, for the night was warm, and the sound of voices came to her at once. Mrs. Palmer had company.

"It 's Miss Presly," said Emarine, resentfully, under her breath. "Old gossip!"

"—goin' to have a fine dinner, I hear," Miss Presly was saying—"turkey with oyster-dressin', an' cran-berries, an' mince-an' punkin-pie, an' reel plum-puddin' with brandy poured over 't an' set afire, an' wine-dip, an' nuts an' raisins, an' wine itself to wind up on. Emarine 's a fine cook. She knows how to git up a dinner that makes your mouth water to think about. You goin' to have a spread, Mis' Parmer?"

"Not much of a one," said Orville's mother. "I expected to, but I c'u'd n't git them fall patatas sold off. I 'll have to keep 'em till spring to git any kind o' price. I don't care much about Christmas, though "—her chin was trembling, but she lifted it high. "It 's silly for anybody but children to build so much on Christmas."

Emarine opened the door and walked in. Mrs. Palmer arose slowly, grasping the back of her chair. "Orville 's dead?" she said solemnly.

Emarine laughed, but there was the tenderness of near tears in her voice. "Oh, my, no!" she said, sitting down. "I run over to ask you to come to Christmas dinner. I was too busy all day to come sooner. I 'm goin' to have a great dinner, an' I 've cooked ev'ry single thing of it myself! I want to show you what a fine Christmas dinner your daughter-in-law can get up. Dinner 's at two, an' I want you to come at eleven. Will you?"

Mrs. Palmer had sat down weakly. Trembling was not the word to describe the feeling that had taken possession of her. She was shivering. She wanted to fall down on her knees and put her arms around her son's wife and sob out all her loneliness and heartache. But life is a stage, and Miss Presly was an audience not to be ignored. So Mrs. Palmer said: "Well, I 'll be reel glad to come, Emarine. It 's offul kind o' you to think of 't. It 'u'd 'a' be'n lonesome eatin' here all by myself, I expect."

Emarine stood up. Her heart was like a thistle-down. Her eyes were shining. "All right," she said; "an' I want that you sh'u'd come just at eleven. I must run right back now. Good night."

"Well, I declare!" said Miss Presly. "That girl gits prettier ev'ry day o' her life. Why, she just looked full o' *glame* tonight!"

Orville was not at home when his mother arrived in her rusty best dress and shawl. Mrs. Endey saw her coming. She gasped out, "Why, good grieve! here's Mis' Parmer, Emarine!"

"Yes, I know," said Emarine, calmly. "I ast her to dinner."

She opened the door, and shook hands with her mother-in-law, giving her mother a look of defiance that almost upset that lady's gravity.

"You set right down, Mother Parmer, an' let me take your things. Orville don't know you're comin', an' I just want to see his face when he comes in. Here's a new black shawl fer your Christmas. I got mother one just like it. See what nice long fringe it's got. Oh, my! don't go to cryin'! Here comes Orville."

She stepped aside quickly. When her husband entered his eyes fell instantly on his mother, weeping childishly over the new shawl. She was in the old splint rocking-chair with the high back. "*Mother!*" he cried; then he gave a frightened, tortured glance at his wife. Emarine smiled at him, but it was through tears.

"Emarine ast me, Orville—she ast me to dinner o' herself! An' she give me this shawl. I 'm—cryin'—fer—joy—"

"I ast her to dinner," said Emarine, "but she ain't ever goin' back again. She 's goin' to *stay*. I expect we 've both had enough of a lesson to do us."

Orville did not speak. He fell on his knees, and laid his head, like a boy, in his mother's lap, and reached one strong but trembling arm up to his wife's waist, drawing her down to him.

Mrs. Endey got up, and went to rattling things around on the table vigorously. "Well, I never see sech a pack o' loonatics!" she exclaimed. "Go an' burn all your Christmas dinner up, if I don't look after it! Turncoats! I expect they 'll both be fallin' over theirselves to knuckle down to each other from now on! I never see!"

But there was something in her eyes, too, that made them beautiful.

THE SURGEON'S MIRACLE

BY

JOSEPH KIRKLAND

"POOR Abe Dodge."

That's what they called him, though he wasn't any poorer than other folks—not so poor as some. How could he be poor, work as he did and steady as he was? Worth a whole grist of such bait as his brother, Ephe Dodge; and yet they never called Ephe poor—whatever worse name they might call him. When Ephe was off at a show in the village, Abe was following the plow, driving a straight furrow, though you wouldn't have thought it to see the way his nose pointed. In winter, when Ephe was taking the girls to singing-school or spelling-bee, or some other foolishness,—out till

after nine o'clock at night, like as not,—
Abe was hanging over the fire, holding a
book so the light would shine first on one
page and then on the other, and he turning
his head as he turned the book, and reading
first with one eye and then with the other.

There, the murder 's out. Abe could n't
read with both eyes at once. If Abe looked
straight ahead he could n't see the furrow —
nor anythin' else, for that matter. His best
friend could n't say but what Abe Dodge was
the cross-eyedest cuss that ever was. Why,
if you wanted to see Abe, you 'd stand in
front of him; but if you wanted Abe to see
you, you 'd got to stand behind him, or
pretty near it. Homely? Well, if you mean
downright "humbly," that 's what he was.
When one eye was in use the other was out
of sight, all except the white of it. Humbly
ain't no name for it. The girls used to say
he had to wake up in the night to rest his
face, it was so humbly. In school you 'd
ought to have seen him look down at his
copy-book. He had to cant his head clear
over, and cock up his chin till it pointed out

of the winder and down the road. You 'd really ought to have seen him; you 'd have died. Head of the class, too, right along; just as near to the head as Ephe was to the foot, and that 's sayin' a good deal. But to see him at his desk! He looked for all the world like a week-old chicken peekin' at a tumble-bug! And him a grown man, too, for he stayed to school winters so long as there was anything more the teacher could teach him. You see, there was n't anything to draw him away; no girl would n't look at him—lucky, too, seein' the way he looked.

Well, one term there was a new teacher come—regular high-up girl, down from Chicago. As bad luck would have it, Abe was n't at school the first week—had n't got through his fall work. So she got to know all the scholars, and they was awful tickled with her—everybody always was that knowed her. The first day she come in and saw Abe at his desk, she thought he was squintin' for fun, and she upped and laughed right out. Some of the scholars laughed too, at first, but most of 'em, to do 'em justice, was a

leetle took back, young as they was, and
cruel by nature. (Young folks is most
usually always cruel—don't seem to know
no better.)

Well, right in the middle of the hush, Abe
gathered up his books and upped and walked
outdoors, lookin' right ahead of him, and con-
sequently seeing the handsome young teacher
unbeknown to her.

She was the worst cut up you ever did see;
but what could she do or say? Go and tell
him she thought he was makin' up a face for
fun? The girls do say that come noon-spell,
when she found out about it, she cried—just
fairly cried. Then she tried to be awful nice
to Abe's ornery brother Ephe, and Ephe he
was tickled most to death; but that did n't
do Abe any good—Ephe was jest ornery
enough to take care that Abe should n't get
any comfort out of it. They do say she sent
messages to Abe, and Ephe never delivered
them, or else twisted 'em so as to make
things worse and worse. Mebbe so, mebbe
not—Ephe was ornery enough for it.

'Course the school-ma'am she was boardin'

round, and pretty soon it come time to go to ol' man Dodge's, and she went; but no Abe could she ever see. He kept away, and as to meals, he never set by, but took a bite off by himself when he could get a chance. ('Course his mother favored him, being he was so cussed unlucky.) Then, when the folks was all to bed, he 'd come in and poke up the fire and peek into his book, but first one side and then the other, same as ever.

Now what does schoolma'am do but come down one night when she thought he was abed and asleep, and catch him unawares. Abe knowed it was her, quick as he heard the rustle of her dress, but there was n't no help for it; so he just turned his head away, and covered his cross-eyes with his hands, and she pitched in. What she said I don't know, but Abe he never said a word; only told her he did n't blame her, not a mite; he knew she could n't help it—no more than he could. Then she asked him to come back to school, and he answered to please excuse him. After a bit she asked him if he would n't come to oblige her, and he said he calculated he was obligin' her more by stayin' away.

Well, come to that, she did n't know what to say or do; so, woman-like, she upped and cried; and then she said he hurt her feelings.

And the upshot of it was he said he 'd come, and they shook hands on it.

Well, Abe kept his word, and took up schoolin' as if nothing had happened. And such schoolin' as there was that winter! I don't believe any regular academy had more learnin' and teachin' that winter than what that district school did. Seemed as if all the scholars had turned over a new leaf. Even wild, ornery, no-account Ephe Dodge could n't help but get ahead some; but then he was crazy to get the school-ma'am, and she never paid no attention to him, just went with Abe. Abe was teachin' her mathematics, seeing that was the one thing where he knowed more than she did—outside of farmin'. Folks used to say that if Ephe had Abe's head, or Abe had Ephe's face, the school-ma'am would have half of the Dodge farm whenever ol' man Dodge got through with it; but neither of them did have what the other had, and so there it was, you see.

Well, you 've heard of Squire Caton, of course; Judge Caton, they call him, since he got to be judge of the Supreme Court—and chief justice at that. Well, he had a farm down there not far from Fox River, and when he was there he was just a plain farmer like the rest of us, though up in Chicago he was a high-up lawyer, leader of the bar. Now it so happened that a young doctor named Brainard—Daniel Brainard—had just come to Chicago and was startin' in, and Squire Caton was helpin' him, gave him desk-room in his

office and made him known to the folks—
Kinzies, and Butterfields, and Ogdens, and
Hamiltons, and Arnolds, and all of those

folks—about all there was in Chicago in
those days. Brainard had been to Paris,—
Paris, France, not Paris, Illinois, you under-

stand,—and knew all the doctorin' there was
to know then. Well, come spring, Squire
Caton had Doc Brainard down to visit him;
and they shot ducks and geese and prairie-
chickens, and some wild turkeys, and deer,
too—game was just swarmin' at that time.
All the while Caton was doin' what law business there was to do; and Brainard thought
he ought to be doin' some doctorin' to keep
his hand in, so he asked Caton if there
was n't any cases he could take up—surgery
cases especially he hankered after, seein' he
had more carving-tools than you could shake
a stick at. He asked him particularly if there
was n't anybody he could treat for "strabismus." The squire had n't heard of anybody
dying of that complaint; but when the doctor explained that strabismus was French for
cross-eyes, he naturally thought of poor Abe
Dodge, and the young doctor was right up
on his ear. He smelled the battle afar off,
and 'most before you could say Jack Robin-
son, the squire and the doctor were on horse-
back and down to the Dodge farm, tool-chest
and all.

Well, it so happened that nobody was at home but Abe and Ephe, and it did n't take but few words before Abe was ready to set right down, then and there, and let anybody do anything he was a mind to with his misfortunate eyes. No, he would n't wait till the old folks come home; he did n't want to ask no advice; he was n't afraid of pain, nor of what anybody could do to his eyes— could n't be made any worse than they were, whatever you did to 'em. Take 'em out and boil 'em and put 'em back if you had a mind to, only go to work. He knew he was of age, and he guessed he was master of his own eyes—such as they were.

Well, there was n't nothing else to do but go ahead. The doctor opened up his killing-tools, and tried to keep Abe from seeing them; but Abe he just come right over and peeked at 'em, handled 'em, and called 'em "splendid"; and so they were, barrin' havin' them used on your own flesh and blood and bones.

Then they got some cloths and a basin, and one thing and another, and set Abe right

down in a chair. (No such thing as chloro-
form in those days, you 'll remember.) And
Squire Caton was to hold an instrument that
spread the eyelid wide open, while Ephe was
to hold Abe's head steady. First touch of
the lancet, and first spurt of blood, and
what do you think? That ornery Ephe
wilted, and fell flat on the floor behind the
chair!

"Squire," said Brainard, "step around and
hold his head."

"I can hold my own head," says Abe, as
steady as you please. But Squire Caton he
straddled over Ephe, and held his head between his arms, and the two handles of the
eye-spreader with his hands.

It was all over in half a minute, and then
Abe he leaned forward, and shook the blood
off his eyelashes, and looked straight out of
that eye for the first time since he was born.
And the first words he said were:

"Thank the Lord! She 's mine!"

About that time Ephe he crawled outdoors, sick as a dog; and Abe spoke up,
says he:

"Now for the other eye, doctor."

"Oh," says the doctor, "we'd better take another day for that."

"All right," says Abe; "if your hands are tired of cuttin', you can make another job of it. My face ain't tired of bein' cut, I can tell you."

"Well, if you're game, I am."

So, if you'll believe me, they just set to work and operated on the other eye, Abe holding his own head, as he said he would, and the squire holding the spreader. And when it was all done, the doctor was for putting a bandage on to keep things quiet till the wounds all healed up; but Abe just begged for one sight of himself, and he stood up and walked over to the clock and looked in the glass, and says he:

"So that's the way I look, is it? Shouldn't have known my own face-- never saw it before. How long must I keep the bandage on, doctor?"

"Oh, if the eyes ain't very sore when you wake up in the morning, you can take it off, if you'll be careful."

"Wake up! Do you s'pose I can sleep when such a blessing has fallen on me? I'll lay still, but if I forget it, or you, for one minute this night, I'll be so ashamed of myself that it'll wake me right up!"

Then the doctor bound up his eyes, and the poor boy said "Thank God!" two or three times, and they could see the tears running down his cheeks from under the cloth. Lord! it was just as pitiful as a broken-winged bird!

How about the girl? Well, it was all right for Abe and all wrong for Ephe—all wrong for Ephe! But that's all past and gone— past and gone. Folks come for miles and miles to see cross-eyed Abe with his eyes as straight as a loon's leg. Doctor Brainard was a great man forever after in those parts; everywhere else, too, by what I heard.

When the doctor and the squire come to go, Abe spoke up, blindfolded as he was, and says he:

"Doc, how much do you charge a feller for savin' his life—making a man out of a poor wreck—doin' what he never thought could

130

be done but by dyin' and goin' to kingdom come?"

"Oh," says Doc Brainard, says he, "that ain't what we look at as pay practice. You did n't call me in; I come of myself, as though it was what we call a clinic. If all goes well, and if you happen to have a barrel of apples to spare, you just send them up to Squire Caton's house in Chicago, and I 'll call over and help eat 'em."

What did Abe say to that? Why, sir, he never said a word; but they do say the tears started out again, out from under the bandage, and down his cheeks. But then Abe he had a five-year-old pet mare he 'd raised from a colt, —pretty as a picture, kind as a kitten, and fast as split lightning,—and next time doc come down, Abe he just slipped out to the barn, and brought the mare round, and hitched her to the gate-post, and when doc come to be going, says Abe:

"Don't forget your nag, doctor; she 's hitched at the gate."

Well, sir, even then Abe had the hardest kind of a time to get Doc Brainard to take

that mare; and when he did ride off, leadin'
her, it was n't half an hour before back she
came, lickety-split. Doc said she broke away
from him and put for home, but I always
suspected he did n't have no use for a hoss
he could n't sell nor hire out, and could n't
afford to keep in the village—that was what
Chicago was then. But come along toward
fall, Abe he took her right up to town, and
then the doctor's practice had growed so
much that he was pretty glad to have her;
and Abe was glad to have him have her,
seeing all that had come to him through
havin' eyes like other folks—that 's the
school-ma'am, I mean.

How did the school-ma'am take it? Well,
it was this way. After the cuttin' Abe
did n't show up for a few days, till the in-
flammation got down and he 'd had some
practice handlin' his eyes, so to speak. He
just kept himself to himself, enjoying himself. He 'd go around doin' the chores, singing so you could hear him a mile. He was
always great on singin', Abe was, though
ashamed to go to singing-school with the

rest. Then, when the poor boy began to feel like other folks, he went right over to where school-ma'am happened to be boardin' round, and walked right up to her, and took her by both hands, and looked her straight in the face, and said:

"Do you know me?"

Well, she kind of smiled and blushed, and then the corners of her mouth pulled down, and she pulled one hand away, and—if you believe me—that was the third time that girl cried that season, to my certain knowledge—and all for nothin' either time!

What did she say? Why, she just said she 'd have to begin all over again to get acquainted with Abe. But Ephe's nose was out of joint, and Ephe knowed it as well as anybody, Ephe did. It was Abe's eyes to Ephe's nose.

Married? Oh, yes, of course; and lived on the farm as long as the old folks lived, and afterward too, Ephe staying right along, like the fool he always had been. That feller never did have as much sense as a last year's bird's nest.

Alive yet?   Abe?   Well, no.   Might have
been, if it had n't been for Shiloh.   When

the war broke out, Abe thought he 'd ought
to go, old as he was; so he went into the

Sixth. Maybe you 've seen a book written about the captain of Company K of the Sixth. It was Company K he went into—him and Ephe. And he was killed at Shiloh—just as it always seems to happen. He got killed and his worthless brother come home. Folks thought Ephe would have liked to marry the widow; but Lord! she never had no such an idea—such bait as he was, compared to his brother. She never chirked up, to speak of, and now she 's dead too; and Ephe he just toddles around, taking care of the children—kind of a he dry-nurse; that 's about all he ever was good for, anyhow.

My name? Oh, my name 's Ephraim—Ephe, they call me, for short; Ephe Dodge. Abe was my brother.

DIKKON'S DOG

BY

DOROTHY LUNDT

THE distinguishing trait of Grubbins was his unexpectedness. Grubbins was Dikkon's dog.

All the cats in the old regiment could have told you that the time it was least safe to try to slip by Grubbins was when he sat gazing across the plains, apparently oblivious of everything on earth but the progress of a mule-train just fading off the distant horizon. The young and untaught kitten who attempted, at such times, to glide with shadow-like swiftness and silence behind Grubbins's meditative back had a never-to-be-forgotten vision of lanky yellow legs lengthening themselves in a leap, bristling yellow hair, and glaring yellow eyes; and if that kitten got off with the loss of his ear or two thirds of his tail, he was congratulated by his more experienced fellows.

Private McAllison was new to the old regiment, which explains his premature assumption that Grubbins was too soundly asleep to resent his tail being stepped on by a friend hastily crossing the barrack-room, or to identify that friend for purposes of reprisal. McAllison was in his stocking-feet, so that his howls, when Grubbins's teeth met through the end of his heel, were louder than they otherwise might have been. Private Mooney, his neighbor of the right-hand cot, gave up in disgust his latest attempt to get sufficiently sound asleep to forget the dismal downpour that was making outdoor life impossible and casting an untimely chill over the twilight of Christmas eve.

"Hould up yer yellin', can't ye, ye Scotch omadahn?" said Private Mooney. "Shure, it's only Grubbins's way!"

"Ma certie! it's a way wull lead Maister Grubbins to the grave that's too lang been

awaitin' him—if not by meelitary execution
by the colonel's orders, then by preevate as-
sassination!" Thus McAllison, with the
polysyllabic solemnity of his nation, nursing
his wounded heel, and glaring at Grubbins,
who had tranquilly returned to his interrupted slumbers.

"I reckon Grubbins's grave ain't dug yet,
nor the man ain't born that 'll send him to
it—not while my name 's Dikkon! Grubbins,
ain't that so, honey?"

The gaunt, yellow dog was alert and on his
feet at the first syllable of his name spoken
in his master's voice. He shambled heavy-
footedly across to the bench where Dikkon
sat, just in from a bit of fatigue-duty at the
stables, toasting his soaked and odorous cow-
hide boots at the low fire in the barrack-room
stove. Grubbins laid his rough, grizzled
muzzle on his master's knee, and Dikkon's
brown and knotted hand fell affectionately
on the dog's head. The two sat looking at
each other with a look of perfect understand-
ing and full companionship. As they sat
thus there was a curious likeness between

man and dog. Dikkon's close-cropped hair was of the same dusty yellow as Grubbins's scraggy coat; chronic malaria and long exposure to every weather had brought Dikkon's complexion to much the same hue that was Grubbins's by birthright; the faded eyes of the man had an expression oddly akin to that which from the dog's eyes looked up at him—a latent gleam through a mist as of habitual drowsy apathy.

"Thet's so, ain't it, honey?" drawled Dikkon again; and Grubbins rapped his stumpy tail in fervent affirmation. "'Pears to me yo' have n't took 's much exercise as common to-day, Grubbins," went on his master. "Don't yo' feel like racin' down a cat or suthin', so 's to get up a moughty good appetite fer yer Christmas grub?"

The men chuckled; the idea of Grubbins's appetite requiring a tonic was a deeply humorous one. Dikkon opened the door, and Grubbins, with a short, approving sniff of the freshening air, trotted loose-leggedly across the soaked parade.

"Shure, it 's an appetite we 'll ahl be

needin' for our Christmas grub," said Private
Mooney, stretching his brawny arms with a
cavernous yawn. "The mule-thrain's over-
due, and divil a thing for Christmas day but
bull-beef an' hardtack, wid likely a redshkin
bullet for sauce wid it!"

"Redskin bullet! Bosh! In midwinter!"
Thus Corporal Perkins, newly from the
Northwest.

"Corporal, me joy, it's forgettin' ye are
that down in this suburb av Tophet there's
niver a winter at ahl, and the redshkins
dishport thimsilves as loively at Christmas
as on the sacrid Fourth o' July! Shure, I
niver pass that clump o' brush beyant the
ould shtables on a black night—an' it's
black nights a-plinty we have, as see the
wan that's a-shuttin' down like a box-lid this
blissid minnit—widout falin' me schalp-lock
a-wigglin' wid spirituous terrors!"

"But the sentries?"

"Faith, it's happened before that the
divil led his own by ways onseen o' the
righteous,—m'anin' Uncle Sam's senthries,
that last,—an' he'll do it ag'in! I say ag'in,

a redshkin bullet 's the Christmas prisint likeliest to come the way av us poor sinners."

"Dikkon, ma lad!" Thus McAllison, stopping by Dikkon's bench to put on his rough overcoat, his injured heel well greased and his Scotch equanimity apparently restored. "I 've nae ill will tae the bit beastie, an' forby he but defendit the richts o' his ain tail. But I 'll gi'e ye a hint for a Christmas gift: it was the colonel himself was sayin' but the nicht's nicht that the next complaint of Dikkon's dog that came tae his ears, the beastie wad ha'e a bullet an' a ditch, an' nae mair said!"

Dikkon sprang to his feet. A dull flush kindled under his yellow skin; the gleam in his faded eyes shone keen through their dulled indifference.

"He will, will he?" There was a savage snarl in the man's voice. "An' what mought *he* be, that 's been with the old regiment only six months, an' not half the use to it then or now that my old dog—"

"Hold hard, Dikkon!" "Whisht, me boy! It 's the short cut to the guard-house you 're takin'!" There were grunts and exclamations of remonstrance on every side. Dikkon looked about him with a sort of bewilderment. The momentary flush and gleam were gone. He sat down again, quietly enough, and put out his feet to the fire.

"Bedad, the colonel's bark is a dale worse nor his bite, we ahl know!" Thus Mooney, pacifically. "It 's only whin his pepper-pot av a timper gits a rough shake that he 's onsafe to play wid. An' Grubbins *is* tryin' at times, his bist fri'nds know. Take it lasht shpring, whin the colonel paid the saints know what ahl for thim seeds from the North; an' whin they was comin' up umbrageous, in sails Grubbins, scoutin' afther a last year's bone he 'd misrimimbered where he 'd buried, an' in tin minnits the colonel's vigitible-garden was plowed up more complate than the field before wan av our batteries at Chattanooga, four years back."

"But that did n't rile him for coppers with Grubbins's gobblin' up little Miss Marion's taffy." Thus Corporal Perkins, picking up his cap, in the general exodus toward the parade. The rain had stopped for a moment. A wild wind was angrily driving the clouds in frightened masses before it. The freshness of the outside world was good to feel, after the stuffy and smoky atmosphere of the barrack-room. "Miss Marion she's the apple o' the colonel's eye, an' the light of it; an' I pity dog or man that sets her cryin' many times as she cried the other day when Grubbins caught on to her taffy the cook had set out to cool, an'—"

"There they go now! See 'em?" Thus one of the men at the window. There was a general turning of heads.

"Faith, it's shmall blame to the colonel," —from Mooney,—"for it's a sunbame little Miss Marion carries in the eyes of her an' the heart of her; an' she kindled it from the wan that wint away wid her mother whin they laid her, an' the ould colonel's heart wid her, in her grave a year gone!"

And indeed three-year-old Miss Marion was a winsome sight to see, as, in her wee blue-hooded rain-cloak, a golden-haired kobold, she danced across the parade by her soldierly grandfather's side, smiling up confidingly in the face that never was stern for her, and leading tenderly, by a ribbon as blue as her rain-cloak or her eyes, a tiny terrier, also blue-blanketed, and mincingly remonstrant at the wet grass that brushed his dainty paws. The men approved of Miss Marion, but the terrier was not regarded with favor in barracks. "For whin I want a dog, I want a *dog*," said Private Mooney, voicing the general sentiment. "An' whin I want a lady-like rat, I don't want him pritindin' to *be* a dog, an' ixpictin' to be rispicted accordin'!"

The men were making their way out for a whiff of fresh air before retreat should sound. Dikkon alone had not left his place by the fire. As Mooney, last of the men, was opening the rough door, he was arrested by Dikkon's voice, sounding musingly and as if unconscious that he spoke aloud.

"It 's a moughty queer world," Dikkon said, "where an old yaller dog will stand to one man for what a pretty little baby does to another!"

With an Irishman's involuntary sympathy for a guessed sorrow, and an Irishman's quick appreciation of a chance to gratify a long-baffled curiosity, Mooney soundlessly closed the door, threw down his cap, and crossed toward an empty chair. After a pause :

"M'anin' yersilf an' the colonel?" said he.

"Meanin' just that. Old Grubbins is about as much to me, I reckon, as little Miss Marion yon is to the old colonel—fer the same reason: all that 's left to me o' somethin' I loved."

Mooney stuffed the tobacco deep into his pipe, and diplomatically waited. There was a momentary break in the heavy clouds, and a late, pale-yellow light shone tremulously through.

"I reckon I never told ye how I met up with Grubbins? I was in the Tennessee mountings, when we wor down there with Grant. That was in '64, years back, when I wor a volunteer. Nigh where we wor camped there wor a cabin. A girl lived there, all alone. Her dad an' five brothers had gone

into the Union army, and they never come
back. Her name wor Marcella. She had
right pretty blue eyes, an' a cough. I
punched a man oncet for tryin' to make
free with her, an' Grubbins chawed him up
afterwards. Grubbins wor her dog—a five-
year-old then, an' 's ornery 's he is now.
We got to be right good friends, she 'n' I;
afterwards, more. I had n't nary a red but
my pay; no more she. But I promised to
come back an' marry her, oncet the fightin'
wor over."

Both men smoked for a time in silence.
"'T was in May, '65, I got back there. It
was a moughty purty day, with clouds like
gold. The cabin do' was tight shet; an' the
windows. Ez I come up I heerd Grubbins
howl. Reckon ye never heerd a yaller dog
howl?

"The neighbors hed jest took care o' her,
an' left her, an' gone back to get the coffin.
She had changed considerable—thin as a
shadder. She had wound grass round my
ring to keep it on her finger. It wor a hoss-
hair ring; I braided it from my hoss's tail.

"I stayed for the fun'ral. Grubbins an' I sot by her all day an' all night. When the grave wor filled in, Grubbins he turned an' reached up his big yaller paw ter me, an' his eyes said, 'Reckon it's we two now, old man?' An' I shuk his paw, an' I says, 'Yes, Grubbins, 's long as we both live.' An' when I 'listed ez a reg'lar, Grubbins 'listed 'long o' me."

"An' wid ahl his ecsyncrasities, Grubbins is a cridit to the ould rigimint!" There was a sympathetic choke in Mooney's voice. "An'—saints be good! phwat 's that?"

It was a wild commotion on the parade-ground. There were growls and snarls and doleful squeals; rushing footsteps, thwacking blows, a child's sobs, a stern and angry voice: "Take that dog away, and—" a short, enraged howl in Grubbins's unmistakable accents.

Dikkon and Mooney were in the middle of the parade. In little Maid Marion's arms, pressed close to her tear-stained face, was a squealing huddle of very muddy blue blanket, with a pathetic pink stain oozing out here and there. Grubbins, his yellow eyes afire, a stout cord round his neck, was in the grasp of a soldier who was vainly trying to combine holding the dog with a respectful salute to his colonel. The colonel's face was gray with rage; his eyes blazed under their shaggy brows. Through the sudden silence Marion's sobs came piteously clear.

"Take away that nasty beast—do you hear?" Thus the colonel, tensely, between his teeth. "I 've overlooked his tricks hitherto, because his master is an old soldier and a good one; but when it comes to killing my granddaughter's pet on the open parade—"

"Shure, the little baste is n't dead at ahl, sorr!" Mooney had gently taken the small blue bundle, separated chewed-up blanket from chewed-up dog, and held the squealing terrier out with one hand, the other at salute, his eyes clouded and anxious. "He 's just dis—disfracshured a bit in shpots, sorr, but a shtrip or two o' plashter 'll make him as good as iver he was, sorr—an' that 's no good at ahl!" jerked Mooney, confidentially, back from his teeth to his throat. "An'

Grubbins mint no harm, sorr. He 'd niver sane the loike before, an' was just investigatin'; an' when he found it wad bite—"

"Hold your tongue, Mooney!" thundered the colonel, recovering the breath that the Irishman's unparalleled audacity had taken away. "Take charge of that dog!" Mooney mechanically took from the soldier the leash at whose other end Grubbins was wildly straining to reach his master. "He has done his last mischief. You will have him hanged within an hour. Not a word, I tell you!"—as Mooney's lips opened in a gasp. "Come, sweetheart." The stern and angry voice fell to a caressing whisper; the colonel lifted Marion, dog and all, and set her on his stalwart arm. "Hush, hush, dear! The bad dog sha' n't hurt little Fido any more. Come home, baby; come and find Christmas." As he turned he stopped abruptly. Dikkon stood squarely facing him. The man's sallow face was dully purple with passion; his eyes gleamed tigerishly. "Take back that order, colonel," he raved. "Give me back my old dog! Give him back, I tell you, or I 'll—"

"Arrest that man!" Dikkon was in the grasp of a dozen ready hands. There was that in his eyes, as they turned on the colonel, that had sent the men's hearts to their throats. "Clap him in the guard-house. He's probably drunk or mad. The court-martial can decide which."

The colonel turned on his heel and strode off through the blackening twilight with the frightened child on his breast. As he went, there followed him the howls of a half-choked dog, as Grubbins was dragged in one direction, powerless to reach the master who was being marched off in the other.

The colonel was in what his sister and housekeeper called a most un-Christmas-like temper throughout his dinner. "Confound the fellow!" he muttered, pacing restlessly to and fro, when dinner was done. "Why need he have given me that madman's talk? Mooney would have found a way to keep the beast safe till the men could send in a petition, and—then—of course—it being Christmas, and all—" He looked abstractedly out into the inky darkness. "Dear, dear! I be-

153

lieve I'm half a madman myself when Marion comes into a question—more than ever since there have been those Apache rumors. I can't leave to carry the child North; and if, while she was here, the Indians—" He put up his hand to his forehead, suddenly damp with the starting sweat.

There rang out through the windy darkness the long-drawn howl of a dog, followed by a sharp, sudden shot, and another and another; shouts, wandering lights.

"What is that? Martha, bar the doors and windows," shouted the colonel, hoarsely. He caught up his sword and buckled it as he ran.

Mooney had come to kindle the smoky lamp in the guard-house cell. The figure lying face downward in the bunk had stirred at sound of his heavy footsteps, and turned toward him a bloodless face and eyes of dumb, agonized entreaty. "Shure, I w'u'd if I c'u'd, ye poor sowl!" said Mooney; yet Dikkon had spoken no word.

"It is n't to let him live. I heard the

colonel's orders. God send him such tor-
ment as he 's sent me! But, Mooney, Grubbins is a soldier's dog. Yo' won't *hang* him?
Oh, for the love o' God, for the sake of
Christmas, *say* yo' won't *hang* him! Yo' 'll
give him a bullet?"

Mooney gripped his hand with a firm, quick
nod.

"I 'm in fo' a term in the military prison,
sho'. Grubbins is gittin' older every day, an'
he 'd be onery, missin' me, an' likely to git
kicked round 'mong the men. He mought
as well go befo' I do. But—yo' 're a good
shot, Mooney, but yo' 'll stand close, an' not
let him need but one bullet?"

Another nod. Mooney shut the door
softly, and went out into the dark. Left
alone, Dikkon threw himself down again in
his bunk, his face hidden in his arms.

"I 'd like to say good-by to yo', Grubbins."
The man was sobbing, thickly, dryly, without
tears. "I 'd have liked to ask yo' to 'a' told
Marcella—"

The long-drawn howl that the colonel had
heard at his window came to Dikkon's ears

as he lay in the guard-house bunk. At the shot that sharply followed the man sat upright, his face gray. "He's gone! The old dog's gone!"

Another shot.

Dikkon leaped up as they say men leap who take a bullet in the heart.

"Mooney! Yo' crazy blunderer! Yo' had to shoot *again!* Oh, my God! Oh, Grubbins! *Grubbins!*"

He flung himself face downward on the floor. He ran his fingers hard into his ears. So he lay, half unconscious, agonized, hearing nothing more.

The colonel stood just without the door of the stables, all the men of the little garrison around and before him. At his feet, across the threshold, lay the body of an Indian, the face taking ghastly cleansing of its war-paint from the thin stream of blood that trickled from its temple. Three other Indians, bound hand and foot, crouched sullenly in the midst of their guard. A trooper was, with many half-choked grunts of discomfort, examining

his shattered knee. The faint, far echo of
galloping ponies was dying away, through the
wind, over the plain.

"Let me understand this," said the colonel.
He spoke somewhat unsteadily. He was looking down at the dead Indian, at whose belt
there dangled a child's scalp. It could not
have been taken many months ago. The
child had had golden hair.

Corporal Perkins stepped forward, salut-
ing. "It was like this, sir. The half-breeds
had probably told them Christmas was a good
time to attack, the men being jolly and care-
less-like. They must have crept up through
the brush behind the stables. There was a
board loose at the back o' the stables; this
fellow"—he indicated the dead Indian—
"crept through it. Their scheme was to
stampede the horses first, so there 'd be no
way of escape. It 'd ha' worked well if—"

"Well?"

"If Grubbins—"

"*Grubbins?*"

"Yis, sorr!"—it was Mooney now, standing sheepish at the salute. "Yer orders was

to hang the dog in an hour, sorr; but when the min was a-thrimmin' the barrack-room clock wid Christmas grane, sorr, they shtopped it intoirely, sorr, an'—"

"Grubbins was in the stables? The dog gave the alarm?"

"Yis, sorr. An' he hild this divil past mischief, sorr, till the senthry—"

"Where is the dog?"

"Shure, he's waitin' his doom, sorr, like his mashter in the guard-house beyant. It's quare they're both in throuble togither,"— Mooney was apparently addressing the universe in general, since he never would have ventured such discourse to his colonel,—"for says Dikkon to me, this afthernoon, says he, 'Grubbins is to me,' says he, 'what the shwate little lady up yonder is to the colonel,' says he—an' little did he think that but for Grubbins, this night, thim divils that's gallopin' away yon might ha' been—this blissid minnit—"

Apparently by accident, Mooney's foot touched the golden hair that fluttered from the dead Indian's belt.

"Release Dikkon!" said the colonel, briefly. There was a queer look in the colonel's eyes. He was very white. "Send him up to me to report. We shall want all our available men before we can round these rascals up."

"Yis, sorr. An' Grubbins, sorr?"

The colonel looked hard in silence at Private Mooney. Then, "Don't you know how to treat the dog that saved the garrison?" said he.

"Yis, sorr. I think so, sorr," said Private Mooney.

The smoky lamp had almost burned itself out.

When a man has his fingers run hard into his ears, how is it any sound can come through? When his eyes are pressed hard against the floor, how can he see great mountains—great mountains, with clouds drifting, majestic, above them; and a homely garden across which the cloud-shadows play; and a girl standing in the garden, with pretty, timid blue eyes up-turned; and an old yellow dog, whining

159

for notice, and importunately licking a man's clenched hands and tear-drenched, hidden face—licking and whining, and shambling eagerly all about a man who lies prone in the dust on the guard-house floor?

"Now I 'm loony for sho'!" Dikkon whispers to himself through closed teeth. "Or p'r'aps it 's his ha'nt. I did n't know dogs had ha'nts. They say ha'nts go away if you speak. I won't speak. I won't open my eyes. It 's 'most as good as 'f they had n't shot him. His tongue 's *warm*. His paw 's *rough*. His nails kin *scratch*. Oh, Lord A'mighty! take him away! take him away! I can't bear anythin' to be so *like* Grubbins when it 's only a ha'nt!"

But the wet tongue caresses; the rough paws plead.

There are footsteps in the room, and lanterns. A dozen comrades are catching at his hand. He has no choice but to sit up and open his eyes.

"Wuz it becos the angels did n't have no wings to fit yo', Grubbins, that they fixed yo' up thataway?" said Dikkon.

160

There, in the full lantern-light, stood an old yellow dog. His neck was hung with Christmas greens. A small American flag was wired to his tail and was wiggling joysomely. His eyes met his master's. With one mighty leap he was in his master's arms, against his master's breast.

"Come away, b'ys," said Private Mooney. "Grubbins 'll be wantin' to exhplain matthers to Dikkon, and, begorra! we 'll be in the way."

THE DIVIDED HOUSE

BY

JULIA D. WHITING

THE DIVIDED HOUSE

*

WHEN Selucius Huxter had arrived at his last illness, he proved himself, more than ever in his life, troublesome and wearing. Having a suspicion that his condition was worse than his doctor or children allowed, he gave them no peace until he had extracted an admission that such was the case. Left alone with the doctor at his request, he reproached him.

"Ye might as well told me before as let me lay here thinkin' and stewin' about it. I 've lost a sight of strength tryin' to git the truth from ye, and there wa'n't no need. Wall—I suppose I ain't reely dyin' naow, while I 'm a-talkin', be I?"

Assured as to that point, he added: "The

165

reason I wanted to know is because I 've got
to fix my concerns so as to leave 'em as well
as I can, and all I want of you is that when
you think I 'm—wall—if you see there 's
goin' to be a change, I want you should tell
me, so 's 't I can straighten things right out,
and git their consent to it."

Having promised, the doctor apprised him
as the last moments drew near.

" Sho! I want to know! Why, I feel full
as well as I did yes'd'y, and a leetle grain
easier, if anythin'."

"I hope this notice does not find you un-
prepared," observed the doctor.

"Wall, no; I 'm prepared as much as I can
be, as you may say. I 've been a member in
good and regular standin' this fifty-five year
—and I hain't arrived at my age without
seein' there 's somethin' in life beside livin'."
He paused, then added with an accent of
pride: "I don't owe any man a cent, nor
never cheated a man of one. Wall, I 've had
quite a spell to think of things in, durin' my
sickness, and I don't know but what I 've en-
joyed it considerable. Thought of things all

along back to when I was a boy. Events come up that I'd clean forgot."

The doctor gone, he called his children in.

"Wall, Armidy, wall, Lucas, the doctor don't seem to think I shall tucker it out much longer. Wall, naow," he exclaimed, quite vexed, "I vow for 't if I did n't forgit to ask him how long! Wall, too late naow. He's got out of sight, I s'pose."

Armida stepped to the window, and assured him of the fact.

"Wall, no gre't matter. I jist thought if I could git him to fix the time I'd like to see how nigh he'd hit it.

"Naow, I want to fix the property so's 't you won't have no trouble with it. No use wastin' money gittin' lawyers here. There ain't no cheatin' nor double-dealin' anywhere to be found amongst the Huxters nor the Lucases; and when you give me your promises to abide by my last will and testament I shall expect you to hold to it jist the same as if it was writ out.

"Naow, about the farm and house. The house, as you know, stands in the middle line

167

of the farm; that is, the north side has a leetle the advantage in hevin' the Jabez Norcross paster tacked unto it, over and above the south half, but it 's near enough. That paster don't count for much; pooty thick with sheep-laurel. Wall, seein' the land lies jist as it does, and the house is jist as it is, I propose to divide it even. Lucas, you can have the north half, and Armidy the south, beginnin' right to the front door and runnin' right through the house and right along down to the river, straight as you can fetch it. Do you agree to my plan?"

Armida and Lucas exchanged glances.

"You speak," said Lucas, in a low tone.

"No, you," said Armida.

"What you whisperin' about? P'r'aps you think I can't hear because I 'm dyin', but I 'd have you to know my hearin' ain't affected a grain. Speak up, naow! What is it, Lucas?"

"We were thinkin' of Theodore," said Lucas. "You 're leavin' him out, seems so."

"'T ain't 'cause I forgot him; but I give him all I cal'lated to when he quit home five year ago—money; and so I sha'n't leave him anythin'. Would n't do him no good, if I did," he said to himself.

"Well, we should feel better if you did," said Armida. "I don't want he should be left out. Neither would mother if she was livin'; she 'd feel bad."

"I 'll settle it with your ma when I see her. Come, naow, what do you say?"

There was a long silence, which Armida broke by saying, "S'posin' him or me was to want to leave the place, I mean for good — get tired of stayin' here to home?"

"Wall," said her father, with a chuckle, "if either of you feels like *givin'* your share to the other, you may. I ain't goin' to leave my old place for either of you to sell to each other nor nobody else. I expect you to live on 't."

"Well," now objected Lucas, "s'posin' one of us should git married, then how would it be?"

"Why, live along. Put in and work a leetle harder, maybe. This farm carried a pooty fair number when I was younger. If you should git too numerous you could build on either side. I guess there ain't no gre't danger," he added.

As neither offered further objections, Mr. Huxter said: "There 's been talk enough, I s'pose. Do you agree to 't?" He waited while each gave an audible " Yes." " Naow," said he, " I hain't an earthly thing to hamper me."

The father dead, for the brother and sister no new life began. Armida still'skimmed all the milk and made the butter and looked after Lucas as she had before, and Lucas attended impartially to the whole of the farm; and Armida sometimes wondered what difference it made. To be sure the profits were divided with the most rigid exactness; but everything went tranquilly on until more than a year after their father's death, when Armida had a suspicion, confirmed by appearances, that Lucas was becoming interested in a young girl in a neighborhood a few miles away. The spirit of jealousy surely animated poor Armida, for nothing else could have prompted her action. Having ascertained the girl's name, she caused to be conveyed

to her the facts, colored for the occasion, relating to the partition of the house and land; and the young woman, having a shrewd eye to the main chance, bluntly told Lucas when next she saw him that she did n't wish the half of a house nor the half of a farm.

Lucas had thought all might go on smoothly with a wife, and had counted on her accepting the situation. Inquiring as to who had meddled in his affairs, he traced the matter back to Armida, and coming home mortified and angry, reproached her in unsparing terms, ending his recital of wrongs with: "I don't know what you did it for, unless you was afraid your half was going to be invaded; and if you feel that way you 'd better keep to your side and take care of your own property. I ain't going to interfere."

Armida was powerless to protect herself except with tears, which did not avail with Lucas. She made overtures of peace, such as offering to cook her brother's meals, and look after his share of the milk, but was warned to attend to her own business.

Lucas had a new pipe-hole made in the kitchen chimney, and bought a new stove, and hunted up a kitchen table, telling Armida she was welcome to the stove and table they had previously used in common, but he 'd thank her to stay on her own side of the room. The situation would have been ludicrous if it had not been grim earnest to the brother and sister. Lucas had a hard side to his character, and he could not forgive his sister's interference. He would not even give Armida advice, but allowed her cows to break into her corn-field and her sheep to stray away, without warning her, though all the while his heart pricked him at sight of her distress. Still all he would do was to suggest that she get a hired man.

Accordingly Armida, in despair, hired an easy-going, good-natured creature that offered his services. He did very well, and Armida got on better and took courage.

But there was a dreadful blow in store for her. Lucas brought a gang of carpenters to the farm, who instituted repairs on his half of the house. He even went so far as to commit the extravagance of having blinds hung for his sitting-room and front-chamber windows, and his half of the front porch was trimmed with brackets, and then the whole of his half of the house painted white, so that his neighbors rallied him on being proud. "Only," as one said, "why don't you extend your improvements right along acrost the house, Lucas? It looks sorter queer to see one half so fine and the other so slack."

"Armida 's free to do she 's a mind to," said Lucas. "If she wants to fix up her side she can. I don't hinder her—"

"Nor you don't help her neither, as I see," said the other.

"I believe in 'tendin' to your own affairs and not interferin' with other folks," Lucas rejoined.

Armida was made very unhappy by these changes, and the comments of the neighbors, and would gladly have beautified her half also, but had no money to spend. The farm had fallen behind and she was pinched for means. She did what she could, taking more care than usual of vines and flowers, and even had an extra bed dug under her front windows, where she had many bright-hued flowers; but as she rose from digging around her plants and surveyed the house—Lucas's side with the new green blinds and the clapboards shining with paint, hers with its stained, weather-beaten appearance and its staring windows—she felt ashamed and discouraged.

She feared her hired man was slack and neglected his work; yet when he threatened to go, and afterward compromised the matter by offering to stay if she'd marry him, she was at a loss what to do, and partly because she was lonely she married him. He was a respectable man, whose only fault was laziness, and she hoped that now he would take an interest. When Armida and her husband came back from the minister's, and announced to Lucas that they were married, his only comment was, "Well, a slack help will make a shif'less husband."

Years went by, and Armida's side of the house fell more and more into ruin, while Lucas, with what Armida considered cruel carefulness, kept his in excellent repair and occasionally renewed the paint. The contrast was so great that passers-by stopped their horses that they might look and wonder at their leisure. Every glance was like a blow to Armida, so that she avoided her sitting-room and kept herself in the uncomfortable kitchen that was divided by an imaginary line directly through the middle, a line never crossed by her brother, her husband, or herself.

It would have looked absurd enough to a stranger to see this divided room, with the brother clumsily carrying on his household affairs on the one side, and the sister doing her work on the other, with often not a word exchanged between them for days together. Absurd it might be, but it was certainly wretched. Armida grew old rapidly. Her husband was a poor stick, and when, as years passed, a touch of rheumatism gave him a real excuse for laziness, he did little more than sit by the fire and smoke.

As Armida sat on the bench under the old russet-apple tree by the back door one day, regretting her evil fate, she heard footsteps

approaching, and, pushing back her old sun-bonnet, looked up to see a shabby, shambling, oldish man coming around the side of the house and gazing in at the windows. "What ye doin' there?" said Armida, sharply.

The man turned, surveyed her with a smile, then said with a drawl she remembered: "I hain't been gone so long but that I know ye, Armidy. Don't you remember me?"

"Theodore Huxter! Is that you? Well!" and she hurried up to him and shook hands violently.

"I heard only last week that father was dead," he explained. "I seen a man from this way, and he said he was gone. How long since?"

"More than ten years ago."

"Well, I thought I 'd come and see ye."

"I 'm glad you did," she said. "But come right in," and she led the way into the kitchen.

He leaned up against the door and surveyed the room. "I should 'a' s'posed I 'd have remembered this room, but what ye done to it? What hev you got two stoves and two tables and all that for, Armidy?"

Armida told him all, winding up her story with a few tears.

"That accounts for the looks of the outside, I s'pose," was his only comment. "I thought it was about the queerest I ever see. It's ridiculous! Why have n't you and Lucas straightened out affairs before this?"

"I can't and he can't, I s'pose," she said hopelessly; "and everything makes it worse. I would n't care so much if he had n't fixed up the outside the way he did."

"Oh, well, now, don't you fret. If I had money—but then I have n't."

"How have you lived sence you left home?" Armida inquired.

"Why, I 've had a still, and made essence, and peddled it out; but I sold the still to git money to come here, and it took all I had."

"Well, now, Theodore, I wish you 'd stay here now you 've got around again," said Armida, with great earnestness. "I 've worried about you a sight. I 'd be glad to have you, and Lucas would, I know."

To spare a possible rebuff for Theodore, she ran out as she saw Lucas coming to the house to get his supper, and apprised him of his brother's arrival, glad to find he shared her pleasure in it. As Lucas entered the room he shook hands with Theodore, saying, " How are ye?" to which Theodore responded with, " How are you, Lucas?"

Theodore was a relief and pleasure to all the family. He observed a strict impartiality. If he split some kindling-wood for Armida, he churned for Lucas. If he took Armida's old horse to be shod, he helped Lucas wash his sheep. He accepted everything, asking no questions after the first evening, but kept an observant eye on all.

Both Lucas and Armida had loved him since their earliest remembrance, and retained their old fondness for him now. He was a welcome guest on either side of the kitchen, and though when he announced of an evening that he was going visiting, and stepped across the line to the other side of the half from where he had been sitting, the owner of the side he honored felt pleased by the distinction, yet the one on the opposite side, though no longer (according to an understood law) joining in the conversation, still had the benefit of Theodore's narratives.

He was busy, too, in his way. He was indefatigable in berry-picking and herb-gathering, selling what Armida and Lucas did not wish, and showing not a little shrewdness. When he had laid a little money together he bought a still, and distilled essences of peppermint, wintergreen, and other sweet-smelling herbs and roots; and when a store was accumulated he filled a basket and departed on a peddling expedition, returning with money in his purse, and a handkerchief or ribbon for Armida. Once he bought her a stuff gown, which she came near ruining by weeping over it, it was such a delight.

Lucas remonstrated. "I think you 're foolish, Theodore. Why don't you spend your money on yourself? You 'd a sight better get you a new coat."

"I 'd rather see Armida cryin' over that stuff," said Theodore, "than have a dozen coats. Nobody knows Armida's good-lookin', because she's no good clothes. But she is, and when she gets that dress made up, and puts it on with that pink ribbon I bought her last time, she'll look as pretty as a pink."

Not so great a success were the Venetian blinds that he bought second-hand and gave to Armida to hang in the sitting-room. They proved to be in sorry condition, and Theodore was much mortified. Being a handy creature, he managed to patch them up so that, though they could not be rolled up, they looked very well from the outside; and, as he philosophically remarked:

"What more do you want, Armidy? A room you never set in you don't want any light in."

There was one thing that Theodore would not do. He would not, as he said, fellowship with Jerry, Armida's husband. "Tell you, Armidy," he would say, "I can't put up with a man like him."

"Some folks call you shif'less, Theodore," Armida retorted with bitterness.

"Well, I am," he allowed; "but the difference is—I'm lazy, but work, my fashion; but he's lazy, and don't work at all."

Though he disdained Jerry, he would rather do his tasks than see Armida's interests suffer, and when he was not occupied with his still or peddling, he busied himself on her side of the farm. Lucas would at any time give him a helping hand rather than see Theodore hurt himself, and so Armida's fences were mended and sundry repairs on her barns and outhouses made. Lucas was still as stiff as ever, and the help given was always to oblige Theodore, who laughed to himself, but said nothing.

He once attempted to wheedle Lucas into painting at least all of the front of the house, but Lucas was not to be moved. Disappointed in that, Theodore brought home a pot of yellow paint when returning from his next expedition, and painted his sister's half of the kitchen floor, in spite of her remonstrating that Lucas would n't like it, though she acknowledged it looked pretty, and in spite of Lucas's vexation at finding the room ridiculous.

"No more ridiculous than it was before," Theodore assured him; "it could n't be. Besides," he added as an afterthought, "I 'll bring it plumb up to the middle, and neither of you will be trespassin' on the other's side. I noticed one of your chairs was a leetle grain onto Armidy's side the other night, and that ain't right."

In the middle of an afternoon, as Lucas was plowing out his corn, he heard a "Hello!" to which, when it had been two or three times repeated, he replied, though without looking around. Presently he heard some one coming, in a sort of scuffling run, and breathing heavily, and looked over his shoulder to see Theodore, who dropped into a walk as he spied him, and gasped: "Lucas! Say! Stop! Look here!"

"Well?" said Lucas, and pulled up his horse.

"I 'm too old to run like this, that 's a fact," said Theodore, mopping his face and leaning up against the plow. "There 's a queer piece of work for us to do, Lucas. Armidy 's all smashed up on the road, right

down here on that second dip, and I guess Jerry is stone dead, and we must fetch 'em up just as soon as we can."

Lucas made no comment, but mechanically unfastened the horse and turned toward the house, his brother stumbling behind, quite exhausted by the hurry and fatigue of the hour.

As they went Lucas said, "How did you come to know of it?"

"Well, it was cur'us," said Theodore. "You know I had old Sam this morning, bringing in a little jag of wood for Armidy, and lengthened out the traces to fit the old waggin. Well, all I know about it is what I guess. I see from the looks they must 'a' concluded to go to the village with some eggs and so on, 'cause you can see in the road where they smashed when the basket flew out; and Jerry did n't know no more than to hitch up into the buggy without shortenin' the traces, and you know how that would work. Well, the cur'us thing is that I was out in the paster mowin' some brakes,—here, let me hitch up this side while you do the

other,—and I heard somebody or somethin'
comin' slam-bang, and I looked up—I wa'n't
near enough so as to see who 't was nor anythin'—and I looked up and see 'em comin'
like hudy down one of them pitches. Thinks
said I, 'Well, there 's a hitchup that 's goin' to
flinders'—and just then the forward wheel
struck a big stone, and I see the woman and
man and all fly inter the air and come down
ag'in, and the hoss went."

"Where 's the horse now?" said Lucas.

"I don't know and I don't care. Tell ye,
best put a feather-bed in the bottom of this
waggin, because her arm 's broke for certain,
and I don't know what else. I 'll fetch it—
if you 've got some spirits."

"Yes," said Lucas, "I 'll fetch some"; and
both hurried into the house and soon came
out again and hastened off.

"How did you know who 't was?" Lucas
inquired, with solemn curiosity fitting the
occasion.

"Why, I did n't; but I knew, when they
did n't offer to git up, whoever 't was wanted
help, and I put across the lot to 'em, and

187

sure enough 't was Armidy and Jerry. I
looked her over, and see by the way she lay
that one of her arms was broke, anyway,
and stepped over to where Jerry was, and,
sir! he was as dead as Moses! Head struck
right on a big stone and broke his neck—his
head hung down like that"—letting his hand
fall limply from the wrist.

"Does she know?" said Lucas.

"No, and I hope she won't for a spell.
She had n't come to when I left her."

Lucas struck the horse with the end of the
reins to urge him on.

"There, now you can see 'em," said Theodore, rising in his seat and pointing down
the road. Lucas followed his example, and
looking before them they could see both
husband and wife lying motionless in the
road.

Between them they soon lifted poor
Armida into the wagon, and laid her on the
bed as tenderly as might be, eliciting a
groan by the operation.

"Best give her some?" said Lucas, bringing a bottle of brandy from out his pocket.

"Come to think of it, best not. She won't sense it so much if she don't realize."

A brief examination of Jerry was sufficient. The brothers exchanged glances and shakes of the head. "And to think," said Theodore, as they regarded the body, "that it was only this mornin' I said to Armidy there was one tramp too many in the house, meanin' me, and now to have my words brought before me like this! 'T was n't anythin' but a joke, but I hope she won't remember it against me."

"Well, first thing we 've got to do is to get her to the house," said Lucas.

Armida having been made as comfortable as the present would allow, and Jerry having been brought up and consigned to the best chamber, as befitted his state, Lucas hastened after the doctor and Aunt Polly Slater. The doctor found Armida in a sad case. "Though I don't think," he assured the brothers, "if she is n't worried she will be hard sick. She 's naturally rugged, and it 's merely a simple fracture of the forearm. The sprained ankle will be the most tedious thing, but I must charge you to keep her in ignorance of her husband's death."

Theodore helped Aunt Polly in caring for Armida, and never was woman more tenderly cared for. Many were the lies he was forced to tell, as Armida was first surprised, then indignant, at Jerry's apparent neglect.

"Even Lucas has come to the door and looked at me," she complained, "and Jerry ain't so much as been near me."

Theodore was fain to concoct a story about a strained back that would not allow Jerry to rise from the bed. When it was deemed prudent to tell her, the task fell to Theodore, who was very tender of his sister, remembering that though he considered Jerry a shiftless, poor shack of a creature, Armida probably had affection for him. She took her loss very quietly.

"He was always good to me," she said, "and he cared for me when no one else did."

"You 're wrong there," Theodore remonstrated.

"I used to tell myself I was," she replied sadly. "I knew I give the first offense, but

Lucas never would 'a' done as he did by the house if he 'd cared for me."

Lucas heard the reproach where he stood out of sight in the little entry that led to Armida's room, listening to the brother and sister as they talked together within. He often lingered there, wishing to enter, but not daring to, longing to atone for the unhappiness he had caused his sister, but not knowing how to set about it. Now, taking Theodore into his confidence, he set to work to obliterate all outward signs that made it "the divided house," leaving to his brother the task of keeping it from Armida. As she querulously inquired what all the hammering and pounding that was going on in front of the house meant, Theodore had a story ready about the steps to the front porch being so worn out that Lucas had to have some new ones, "or else break his legs goin' over them." The smell of paint was accounted for by Lucas's "havin' one of his spells of gittin' his side painted over ag'in," on which Armida gave way to tears, until her brother comforted her by saying it did n't make much difference; a new coat could n't make it any whiter than it was.

It was a great day when Armida was pronounced well enough to eat breakfast in the kitchen. Hobbling out with the aid of Theodore's arm, she stepped on the threshold, and looked over to where Lucas stood by his window. He greeted her with, "How are ye, Armidy?" but did not leave his place.

"It seems good to git out of my bedroom," said Armida, then stopped, gazed about her, and sank into a convenient chair, exclaiming, "What does it mean?"

For both her and Lucas's old stoves were gone, and a new one stood directly before the middle of the chimney, with its pipe running into the old pipe-hole that they used before the house was divided. The coffee-pot steamed and bubbled over the fire, and a platter of ham and eggs stood on the hearth, while the table, set for breakfast, stood exactly in the center of the room. The dividing line had been wiped out by the paint-brush, and Lucas's side shone with yellow paint like her own.

"What does it mean?" she cried, trembling and clutching at Theodore's arm. Theodore said nothing, but slipped out of the room; and Lucas, after an awkward pause, said: "Armidy, I wanted, if you was willin', that we should quit doin' as we have done, and have things together as we used to. Seems as if it would be pleasanter, and if you can forgive what I 've done, I 'll try to make it up to ye."

"Why, Lucas!" was all she could say.

"I know I hain't done by ye like a brother," said Lucas, anxious to get his self-imposed humiliation over, "and I 'm sorry, and I 'd like to begin over again."

"I 'm just as much a transgressor as you be," said Armida, anxious to spare him. "If I had n't said what I did, I s'pose you 'd married Ianthe, and like as not had a family round ye."

"I don't know as I care *now*," said Lucas; "I have felt hard to ye, but I see Ianthe last March"—he laughed—"and I did n't mourn much that her name wa'n't Huxter. But that 's neither here nor there. If you feel

as if you could git along with two old
brothers to look after instead of one, and
overlook what 's passed—"

"I 'd be glad to, Lucas, if you won't lay
up anythin' against me."

"Well, then," and coming to her side
Lucas bent over her, and, to her great sur-
prise, kissed her. Turning away before she
could return the kiss, he opened the back
door and called to Theodore.

As Theodore came in Lucas said: "If you
had a shawl round ye, Armidy, would n't you
like to git out a minute before breakfast?"
and without waiting for an answer he
brought her shawl and wrapped it round
her, then put on her bonnet.

"Can't you and I," he said to Theodore,
"make a chair and take her out? You hain't
forgot sence you left school, hev you?"

Locking their hands together, they formed
what school-children call a chair, and lifting
Armida between them, carried her through
the hall, out at the front door, down the
walk to the gate, and turned round, while
Theodore bade his sister look up at the

house.   Armida obeyed.   She saw the house glistening with paint, her side of it as white as Lucas's, and blinds adorning her front windows, while the front porch, with new-laid floor and steps and bristling with brackets, was, in her eyes, the most imposing of entrances.

Could it be true? she asked herself, and shut her eyes; then glanced again, then looked at her brothers, who were both silent, Theodore smiling with joy, while Lucas looked gravely down at her.

"Oh, Lucas!" she cried, throwing her arms around his neck, "you done this for me!"

"I *told* you I was sorry, Armidy," he said.